"Let me tell you one of Father Murphy's many quotes,"

Phillipa said. "'An archaeologist is the best husband a woman can have. The older she gets, the more interested he is in her.'"

A perfunctory smile crossed Gile's face. "I'm a modern man, Phillipa. I cannot and will not accept the double standards of—"

"Of what?" she asked sardonically. "Of my generation?"

"Of others," he said harshly. "Why should an older woman be different from an older man?"

Her voice was low, barely above a whisper. "Because I'm supposed to be your sister. And that is the only relationship we can possibly share."

She left, but he caught up with her outside the *taverna* and blocked her way, his hands braced against the wall at either side of her head. "All right, love. I'll play by the rules I agreed to. I'll be your loving brother—" his head bent, and his lips brushed her cheekbone "—for now."

Dear Reader,

When two people fall in love, the world is suddenly new and exciting, and it's that same excitement we bring to you in Silhouette Intimate Moments. These are stories with scope, with grandeur. These characters lead the lives we all dream of, and everything they do reflects the wonder of being in love.

Longer and more sensuous than most romances, Silhouette Intimate Moments novels take you away from everyday life and let you share the magic of love. Adventure, glamour, drama, even suspense— these are the passwords that let you into a world where love has a power beyond the ordinary, where the best authors in the field today create stories of love and commitment that will stay with you always.

In coming months look for novels by your favorite authors: Maura Seger, Parris Afton Bonds, Elizabeth Lowell and Erin St. Claire, to name just a few. And whenever you buy books, look for all the Silhouette Intimate Moments, love stories *for* today's women *by* today's women.

Leslie J. Wainger
Senior Editor
Silhouette Books

IMRL-7/85

Parris Afton Bonds

Wanted Woman

Silhouette Intimate Moments

Published by Silhouette Books New York

America's Publisher of Contemporary Romance

SILHOUETTE BOOKS
300 East 42nd St., New York, N.Y. 10017

Copyright © 1987 by Parris Afton Bonds

ISBN: 0-373-07189-2

First Silhouette Books printing May 1987

America's Publisher of Contemporary Romance

Printed in the U.S.A.

PARRIS AFTON BONDS

has been writing since she was six, though she didn't turn professional until her family moved to Mexico. She gives the credit for her several literary awards to her husband and sons, who have given unstintingly of their love and support.

For Cory Kenyon
Two souls who know the true value of
Trivial Pursuit and horse racing

Chapter 1

The gray Welsh wind howled through the Druid-drowsy woods and across a country haunted by the myth of Camelot. Like the hounds of hell, the mid-summer wind swept down over the pastoral heartland of Wales, the land of bards, where thirty stalwart Welshmen waged nonstop unarmed combat.

Though wearing shinpads and rugby shorts, with sweat staining his kelly-green team shirt, the fourth and only surviving son of Baron Hayes-David exuded an aura of *arbiter elegantiae*, a man who was in control of even the most minute details of his image. Tall, nearly six foot three, Giles Hayes-David possessed a young god's face and an extraordinary male physique, honed by those sports that build the kind of long, ropy muscles that make a couturier purr. Wide of shoulder and narrow of hip, his lithe body usually moved with the assurance and dark grace of a bullfighter.

That afternoon, however, he strode off the field with an almost imperceptible limp that attacked his left leg only when he was deeply fatigued. A circle of congratulatory country squires welcomed him in the eloquent offspring of the Celtic language spoken at King Arthur's legendary court—*Croeso...Saeson... Meysydd Hela cŵn Brenin Annwn...Ogof Ddu... Llaethnant.*

A lovely redheaded young woman dressed in an Italian designer's creation insinuated herself into the masculine domain and clasped Giles's arm, giving it an adoring squeeze. Beneath marvelously thick brows her hazel-green eyes roamed over his pure profile with something closer to possessiveness than pride. Gwynfor, whose family estates adjoined his, had had a crush on him since she was a child, even though he was a full eight years older. "You were wonderful, Giles!"

He glanced down at Gwynfor and smiled wearily. "You are prejudiced, I hope."

By the same time next year, when the Welsh heiress turned twenty-five, she would become his bride, ensuring both the continuation of their Welsh bloodlines and the transfer of her financial assets to his brooding estate, Cambria.

At the present moment he was interested in neither his fiancée's Welsh blood nor her Evans Woolen Mills' money. He felt strangely discontented and wanted only to escape to solitude for a while.

Gwynfor, on the other hand, was very much interested in him—and his tattered title, if she was to be
honest about it—and wanted him with her.

"Let me shower," he told her, "then we'll enjoy a
drink before motoring back to Caernarvon."

The gym's shower doused him with splinters of cold
water, restoring his vigor, but not his contentment. In
his heart he knew his dissatisfaction stemmed from
discovering the existence of something he had been
unaware he was lacking: the spark between two souls.
On his odyssey to the Arab emirate of Baghrashi weeks
earlier he had been so aware of the magical chemistry
between his friend and past employer, Khalid Rajhi,
and the lovely American divorcée, Alyx Langford.
Giles knew he had never experienced such a feeling and
probably never would.

Despite its location in a pocket of Methodist tem-
perance, the local pub fared well. There was a warm
and smoky ambience inside the white-stucco and black-
trimmed Tudor building known simply as St. David's.
Giles chose a table near the single bottle-glass window. A childhood spent in the bowels of a black
mountain had left him with a mania for light and color.
A buxom barmaid brought him a pint of porter and,
for Gwynfor, a glass of sherry drawn from an ancient
cask of Amontillado.

Gwynfor smiled at him over her amber liquor. "I can
hardly wait for our wedding, darling." But her eyes

said to him, You have escaped me too many times, my arrogant stallion.

"To us," he said, very much aware of her romantic infantile machinations. Then he felt an angry impatience at the discontent that plagued him. Gwynfor had absolutely no depth, but she would make a perfect wife.

That night Gwynfor offered herself to him in a room above St. David's. She wasn't a virgin, though she coyly attempted to convince him otherwise. Her lack of maidenhead made no difference to him, but he found her subterfuge rather irritating. Without wanting to dwell on their lovemaking—if it could be called that, he thought grimly—he knew that he was treading the well-worn, guilt-ridden path of compromise.

What the bloody hell, by tomorrow he would be on his way to a new country and a different kind of assignment.

He belonged to someone else, and there wasn't a damned thing, Lady Phillipa Fleming told herself, she could do about her quiet, unrequited passion for Macedonia's brilliant leader. Damon Demetrios had pledged his heart to Sigourney Hamilton and made the world-famous journalist his. The only competition Macedonia's first lady might have came from Macedonia itself.

Phillipa had merely to look down the length of the dinner table, past myriad Macedonian cabinet heads, to see raven-haired Sigourney, dressed in a vibrant, lacquer-red Saint Laurent creation. Phillipa, wearing a high-necked black jersey Givenchy with a white lace collar and cuffs, felt positively Victorian.

As hostess for that evening's cabinet dinner at the National Palace, Sigourney radiated a youthful, vital energy. Under the prismed light of the crystal chandeliers her Eurasian beauty overshadowed that of the other women present, like a bonfire in the midst of candles. To make matters worse, Phillipa couldn't even enjoy the luxury of green jealousy. Sigourney Demetrios was a dear and valued friend.

With an audible sigh of heartache Phillipa pulled her gaze away from Sigourney, only to lock eyes with the guest of honor on her right, the impeccably dressed young man who, according to their covering story, was her younger brother. In his hard, clean-cut face, Giles Hayes-David's mouth quirked in the slashing line of a spectator's amusement. Had the tawny-haired young Welshman guessed her shameful secret? Was her repressed love for Damon Demetrios that evident in her smoothly controlled features?

She barely managed a sisterly smile for the young, former British Secret Service agent, who just that morning had officially been hired by Damon to act as director for Macedonia's governmental reconstruction projects. Out of the ruins created by the tyrannical General Agamemnon's toppled regime, Damon's Pan-Hellenic administration hoped to lift Macedonia to the status befitting the country that had once been the cradle of democracy and intellectual civilization.

"You look rather tired, love," Giles said in English, draping his arm over the back of her chair in an affectionate, brotherly gesture.

Of course she looked tired! She was forty-six years old to his thirty-two—or whatever age Giles had claimed at their briefing session that morning with Damon. She mustn't forget details like that.

Odd, she hadn't cared about aging when Aaron had been alive. Then, after one of Agamemnon's henchmen had assassinated her husband, she had gone underground, working with Damon and his Pan-Hellenic Free Forces. The strain of leading a double life and the horrors she had seen and undergone at the infamous Toridallos Prison had left their mark on her soul, if not her features. With Aaron she had known love, a strong love born not of passion but rather of trust and friendship. Now, at her age, she doubted she would ever experience love again.

"I suppose I am a little tired," she murmured, taking a sip of the Veuve Clicquot champagne. She was damned tired of waiting for whatever crumbs of Damon's attention she could pick up.

On her left Macedonia's minister of justice, the swarthy Gregorios Zychapoulos, leaned over and said unctuously, "It must have been an exciting and busy day for you, Lady Phillipa, meeting your brother for the first time in—how many years did you say?"

"She is exhausted," Giles interjected smoothly in rusty, Welsh-accented Greek. "We both are."

"President Demetrios seems to have a great deal of confidence in your abilities, Sir Robert," persisted Zychapoulos, who reminded Phillipa of a shriveled olive. "What did you do in England?"

She took a fortifying sip from her Baccarat balloon glass. Her chilled fingers clutched the stem, waiting for Giles's reply. There had been so little time that morning to coach him in family history, and Zychapoulos had been acquainted with her mother's family before her mother had married the Earl of Innes and moved to England. How much did the old man recall about her mother's marriage?

"I was the adviser on the Rothingham properties and the projects of our older brother, Guy," Giles said easily in that marvelously rich voice with which all Welshmen seemed blessed. "But I wanted to do something on my own, and this position in Constantine presented the perfect opportunity."

Some of the tension ebbed from Phillipa, at least for the moment. She must have been a fool to have given in to Damon's request. But then, she could deny the big blond Macedonian nothing, although she had tried time and again to expel him from her heart.

She had been prepared to leave Macedonia for good, to return to her ancestral estate in Berkshire before either Damon or Sigourney could suspect the depth of her agony, when Damon had asked her to work on one last operation with a man who was a younger version of himself, but who, as it turned out, was merely a mercenary, selling his expertise to the highest bidder.

At last Sigourney laid her napkin next to her plate, signifying that the cabinet dinner was at an end. Gratefully Phillipa rose from the high-backed chair Giles pulled out for her. "Thank you for a lovely evening, Sigourney," she told her friend.

"You two are not staying for an after dinner drink?" asked Major Veranos. The bland-looking man, whose nondescript brown eyes were nonetheless alert, was Damon's internal security commander.

"Not tonight," she said. She managed to look up fondly into Giles's sea-blue eyes, which were watching her, watching everything and everyone, actually. If the report Khalid Rajhi had given Damon was accurate, the mind of the dispassionate Welshman worked in fast forward. "My brother and I have a lot of reminiscing to do, Major."

Sigourney kissed her warmly on the cheek. "I can understand, dear." She flashed a smile at Giles. "I'm so pleased you decided to accept Damon's job offer. Phillipa needs a loving eye to watch over her."

Some of Giles's cool, contained manner softened before the first lady's vivacious youthfulness. "The pleasure is all mine, Mrs. Demetrios."

"The weekend is also yours," Damon said, a smile easing his battlefield-handsome face. "Then we put you to work for Macedonia."

Giles was already secretly at work for Macedonia— and Damon, Phillipa thought. Then she forgot everything as Damon gave her a light kiss on the lips. The effect was like a nail driven into her heart.

As hastily as was discreetly possible, she made her farewells and departed with Giles. She was thankful for his firm, supportive hand at the small of her back as he guided her down a marble corridor, flanked at intervals by blue-and-white-uniformed guards.

Once she was inside the sleek white Mercedes stretch limousine Damon had provided, her body went limp, as if her bones had turned to liquid. She sank back into the blue velour seat, her head resting on its back, and closed her eyes. How much longer would she have to carry out this latest deception?

The oh-so-proper Lady Phillipa Fleming, offspring of a Macedonian industrialist's daughter and an English earl, was worn close to the breaking point by years of working covertly as an operative for Damon—and years of concealing the ineffable pain of her love for him under the guise of a longtime devoted and loving friend.

Beside her, Giles pushed one of the buttons on the armrest, and a panel ascended, effectively separating the passenger compartment from the chauffeur.

"Now, who is this Zychapoulos?" Giles asked in a clipped, efficient tone. "Besides being Macedonia's minister of justice?"

Grudgingly she opened her eyes. She didn't like talking to anyone lately. She was disturbed that her basic emotion was anger—anger directed at herself. Was that the reason behind her recent appetite for silence?

"Gregorios Zychapoulos is a former member of the more radical Macedonian Provisional Army that sought Agamemnon's overthrow through terrorist acts."

"I understand the MPA is now striving to overthrow Damon's Pan-Hellenic government."

"Yes, but Gregorios was one of the MPA's more conservative members. That's why, after Damon was elected president, he appointed Gregorios to his cabinet, as a conciliatory gesture. How did you learn Greek?"

"Rather Neanderthal, isn't it? I spent the summer of my sophomore year at the university here in Constantine as an exchange student."

"Then you probably knew my..."

"Who?"

She had almost told him about Aaron, who had been president of the university when Agamemnon had overthrown the monarchy, but then she would have had to explain about Aaron's murder just prior to the revolution, and she didn't want to reimmerse herself in any of the hideous details.

"It's not important. What if Gregorios checks up and finds that my younger brother, Robert, is alive and well elsewhere?"

"Both your brothers have agreed to cooperate with our cover story. Hopefully, if—and by the time—any in-depth research is conducted into your family history, I will have discovered the identity of the MPA's Oracle of Delphi."

The Oracle of Delphi, as Phillipa and a few others who were trusted by Damon had learned, was the code name used by a traitor in a communique intercepted by Damon's internal security division. "You think Gregorios could be the one betraying state secrets to the MPA? You think he is the Oracle?"

In the dark of the limo, Giles's eyes glittered glacial blue. "I think anyone could be the mysterious traitor seeking to topple Macedonia's Pan-Hellenic government, including yourself, dear sister Phillipa." He took her hand and squeezed it in a gesture of mock affection.

Pulse racing, she jerked her hand away. He reminded her a bit too much of Damon; there was their golden coloring, of course, though Giles was leaner and much younger. There was also their aura of detached self-command. But the undercover agent had none of Damon's dedication to his country.

Disgust left a metallic taste on her tongue. "I applaud your openmindedness, but you don't have to carry on the farce of brotherly love when we're alone, Mr. Hayes-David!"

"Bobby, dear sis," he reminded her.

She said nothing, just stared dismally out the window as the capital's suburbs slid into night-darkened countryside. Tucked into the rolling hills of the Rhodope Mountains was the centuries-old Villa Arcadia—the name the ancient Spartans had given to the picturesque mountain region. Soon after Damon had been elected president he had returned to Phillipa her mother's sprawling family estates, which Agamemnon had confiscated. Its stables had once been famed for their Thoroughbreds, but those had been sold off long ago. Now she kept only four horses for herself and her occasional guests.

The stone-faced Daphne, who had been with Phillipa since her marriage to Aaron and who supervised a staff consisting of a chambermaid, cook, groom and two gardeners, opened the door to her and Giles. "Daphne," Phillipa said, raising her voice to the near-deaf old woman, "this is my brother Robert. You've heard me talk about him."

Daphne's impassive features softened as much as her time-worn flesh would permit. "Yes, my lady."

"He will be staying until . . . until we can find suitable living quarters for him in the city."

"Yes, my lady."

Giles followed Phillipa up the wide, red-carpeted staircase and along a vaulted hallway, cool despite the heat of the July evening. Ancestral portraits and blank-eyed statues watched the villa's newest guest pass by.

"How many rooms?" he asked casually.

"I'm not sure, really," she said, slightly amused that she couldn't answer the question. "I've tried to count them, but I always run into the problem of what qualifies as a room. There are rooms, for instance, solely for flags. Do I count them? And what about bathrooms? Do they count? My grandfather had a room just to store his shoes. Does it count? Really, I don't know how many rooms—maybe somewhere around seventy-five.

"This will be your room," she said, opening a nail-studded door into a guest suite done in shades of persimmon and oatmeal.

Hands in his trouser pockets, front panels of his black dinner jacket shoved back, Giles strode around the room like a master surveying his domain. The villa might have been sixteenth century, but the furnishings were spare and modern: a chrome, brass and glass coffee table; a deco-pop sofa; a king-size bed in one corner, opposite a fireplace of Carrera marble designed in unaffected lines.

At last he turned to look at her. "Ahh, the pleasures of the simple life."

"You don't approve?"

He glanced negligently around again; then his assessing gaze returned to her. "I am also the beneficiary of a *simple* little estate. Mine is in Wales—Cambria, a gloomy monolithic castle on five thousand acres. Bloody problem is, the place is running to seed. I could easily spend twenty-five thousand pounds a year just on the upkeep of the grounds."

"Which is why you are...doing this type of work?"

"Precisely. It's the old stiff upper lip and all, old girl," he joked.

Old girl. He was closer to the target than his careless words implied, she thought disagreeably.

He flicked a pointed glance at one of the diamond drops glistening at her earlobes. "I would imagine the outlay for that little bit of jewelry could easily equip Macedonia's impoverished army.''

"I doubt that seriously!'' She fairly bristled at the young man; he seemed so self-sufficient, so arrogantly male. "Tomorrow you may stroll around our grounds, prowl through our closed-off rooms, observe the rooms open to the public. Your operative's keen eyes will no doubt note that everything is a little shabby, a bit frayed. But as far as Macedonia's proud citizens are concerned, I am one of the last of its illustrious, aristocratic breed—and one of the last people who would be suspected as a traitor!''

"And one of the last people suspected of being one of those feminist warriors who would gladly lay down her life for the heroic Damon.''

Anxiously she glanced up into the ascetic blue eyes of the Welshman. "Why do you say that?''

He ambled across the Westminster carpet to stand before her, and she suppressed the instinctive urge to shrink away from his invasion of her territory. Had this upstart never learned to respect his elders? Nevertheless, her gaze skidded elsewhere, to settle at last on his black bow tie.

"Oh, do come on, Lady Phillipa,'' he drawled in what seemed a careless tone. "I'm one of your own kind, remember? We are both a lot alike. Impoverished British subjects parading as affluent aristocracy. Now why is it I suspect there is nothing you'd like better than to lay down your starving body for him?''

Her head lifted with exaggerated slowness, as if she couldn't believe his audacity. "I think you had better retire for the night!"

He laughed outright, a full-bodied masculine laugh. "Why, you're almost snarling, *Lady* Phillipa. Imagine that! The sedate noblewoman, who would never have the courage to think or do anything improper, sinking to such a bourgeois action. Tell me," he said, in a too-idle voice that caught her off guard, "how long has it been since you've known what it is to be a woman, wholly and fully?"

For the first time in a long while she felt light and alive with her anger and recklessness. "*You* are a chauvinist—a crude one, at that—stunned with hormones and ambition, who hasn't even really lived yet!"

A smile of surprise lifted the corners of his boyish mouth, but his manner became businesslike. "You're quite right. I'm not usually so rude. But if I'm to work with you, to place my life in jeopardy, I have to know your weaknesses and your limits. Women are, I find, too emotional for this type of work."

So he had been testing her. She stalked to the door. Opening it, she looked over her shoulder at him and, fighting for control and composure, said clearly, steadily, "My emotions haven't always been so apparent. Only recently have I...let down my guard. I promise you, I won't be so weak in the future."

She could see the skepticism in his eyes, but he merely said a little more kindly, "You *are* tired. Get some sleep. Tomorrow both of us will feel better."

She closed the door behind her. Spasms of weariness robbed her legs of their normal strength, and only her hands on the doorknob at the small of her back supported her weight. The Welshman was right. She was tired, but she doubted if she would feel any better tomorrow.

These days her thirst for complicity, for the sense of danger and intrigue as an outlet for her untapped sexual drive, did not seem to be enough. Some women channeled their repressed desires through other outlets: their children, or numerous charity and social organizations. Others lived for chocolate or martinis, and still others for drugs to provide an escape.

She thought of all her fruitless, arid, passionless nights. She had thought she had long ago extinguished her emotions, but it appeared as though some ember had survived to occasionally torment her with her latent sexuality and remind her of her flickering feminine needs.

Chapter 2

So it's to be a small, intimate dinner this evening at the home of Macedonia's vice president?"

Keeping her eye on Constantine's crowded boulevard, Phillipa nodded. Negotiating the ivory white BMW 325e through the capital's rush-hour traffic was a death-defying act. Doubtless the competent Giles Hayes-David would be relieved when Damon came through with the governmental car promised to all state employees.

"Sotoris Lazeros is Damon's most trusted confidant," she said, filling Giles in on the background of the vice president. "He served as a freedom fighter under Damon and eventually had to flee with his family to the island of Rhodes, where he and his wife, Sophie, continued to work for the overthrow of Agamemnon's regime."

"Even so, just how trustworthy is this Sotoris Lazeros, Lady Phillipa?"

She flicked a cursory glance at the immaculately donnish stranger in the seat next to her. Giles invariably dressed as if he had just stepped off Savile Row. Damon could never have worn such clothes with the élan Giles did. Giles no doubt spent several thousand pounds on clothes each year, and tried on as many as three or four shirts before settling on the one he was willing to be seen in that evening, all to create a sophisticated image to deceive the public.

She was dressed tastefully in a tailored two-piece gray linen suit with a frothy raspberry raw silk blouse. Yes, she and this illusionary brother were, as he had so carelessly pointed out, a lot alike. It seemed as if she had known him for more than a mere two days.

"Sotoris and Sophie risked their lives for Damon over and over," she said dryly. "I think that is sufficient evidence of the vice president's trustworthiness."

"No, it is not. Even a taste of power can corrupt. You are too trusting, Lady Phillipa."

"Do you trust no one?"

"No one."

"For a man so young, you are far too cynical."

"You make me sound young enough to be your son."

A rueful smile brought out the attractive laugh lines the years had given her. "You almost are." She glanced in the rearview mirror and combed her fingers through her stylishly cut, short blond hair that was gradually being invaded by silvery strands. "I believe Damon said you worked for Khalid Rajhi's father in Baghrashi, is that right?"

"You knew Khalid?"

"Yes. We worked together for almost a year as freedom fighters. Was he the one who told you about the Pan-Hellenic movement?"

"Only about Damon's effort to reestablish democracy here in Macedonia. And then I was introduced to Father Murphy when he was in Baghrashi. It was Father Murphy who convinced both me and Damon that I could be helpful in discovering the traitor."

"Father Murphy—one of my favorite people!" Giles chuckled. "A gunrunning, quote-loving priest. What a paradox."

"Father Murphy is one of the ugliest and at the same time most beautiful human beings I have ever met." She pointed to her left. "We're here."

Sotoris and Sophie lived, along with their two daughters, in a suburb that included the more affluent Embassy Row, a section occupied mostly by foreign diplomats. The Lazeros home, however, was a simple two-story building whose sunbaked outer walls were the time-enriched color of terra cotta. Sotoris and Sophie were much the same, Phillipa had always thought—two earthy people whom time had enriched.

Sophie greeted them at the door. The big-boned peasant woman gave Phillipa an affectionate hug and kissed her on each cheek. "We've missed you lately!"

"I've been caught up with Robert's arrival. Sophie, this is my younger brother, Robert Bowmont."

Shyly, Sophie shook his hand. "My husband has told me much about you, Sir Robert."

"Robert, please."

Her wide mouth dimpled in a smile. "Robert. Sotoris says that you are already one of the hardest workers at the National Palace."

Giles smiled politely. "That's because Damon drives me mercilessly."

"I've brought something for the girls," Phillipa said. "The latest in talking dolls. I understand they're the rage in the United States and England right now. Where are they?"

Sophie rolled her eyes. "Upstairs with their father. Sotoris offered to bathe them while I finished cooking dinner, but he makes a bigger mess than they do! Water everywhere. Half a dozen towels scattered over the floor." She tossed her head upward in Greek fashion. "Men! Baah!"

Over *domaldes*, tender grape leaves stuffed with meat and rice, and a bottle of the ubiquitous native retsina, for which Phillipa had never acquired a taste, the conversation flowed easily. Sotoris, a small, wiry man with an impressive mustache, attempted to explain to Giles some of the problems Macedonia's new government faced.

"When Pan-Hellenic took over the government's reins, the economic state of the nation was disastrous. Agamemnon had been spending hundreds of millions of drachmas to keep up his fantastic life-style while the countryside was in the throes of starvation. Some of our people expected immediate results from Damon. Correcting problems that took a dozen years to form is not something that can be done in a month—or even a year."

Sotoris's two daughters, who couldn't have been more than eight and nine, twisted restlessly in their chairs, except when Giles directed a charming glance in their direction. "He looks like Uncle Damon, doesn't he, Mommy?" the eldest, a curly moppet, asked.

"Why, yes, he does."

"Except," Giles said, with a wink for the two girls, "I'm not as strong."

"And Damon is married," the youngest chipped in. Her saucer-wide eyes stared at him with anxious intent. "You're not, are you?"

"No, I'm not. As pretty as you are, I would certainly be willing to wait for you to grow up."

Both girls giggled behind pudgy hands. Sophie and Sotoris exchanged warm glances that spoke of their mutual pride in their children, of their own closeness, of their commitment to each other and to life. Theirs was a love that seemed to Phillipa almost spiritual. Envy pricked her, but she reminded herself that she alone was responsible for her life; she had made her choices. At her age one didn't look back with regrets, only ahead...except that she had no enthusiasm for the future these days.

After a while Giles excused himself from the table, ostensibly to go to the bathroom. Now it was Phillipa's turn to keep the conversation active so Giles's inordinately long absence would not be noted. She felt disloyal to the Lazeroses, two nice people who loved Macedonia as much as she did.

Or who *seemed* to, as far as Giles was concerned. At that moment he was most likely installing a direct tape to the basement's telephone bridge box, attaching a set of wires that ran into a pocket-size tape recorder that would be concealed nearby.

More than ten minutes passed, and she was beginning to get nervous. Dear God, why had she agreed to continue such a stress-filled way of life?

Because you would do anything for Damon, a small voice whispered.

A moment later Giles reentered the dining room, looking calm. "Quite an amazing assortment of seashells you have in the bathroom, Mrs. Lazeros," he said easily.

No wonder, Phillipa thought testily, Father Murphy had recommended Giles. His calm was unflappable. She found it vexing to live in close quarters with a man she found both cocky and calculating. His display of attentiveness toward the Lazeros daughters had been initiated, she suspected, for no other reason than to gain the family's trust.

Perhaps she was misjudging him, but in her line of work she had long ago learned never to trust anyone on face value. A wrong judgment could mean the difference between success and failure, life and death.

"My daughters collected the shells from the beaches when we lived in Rhodes," a pleased Sophie told Giles. "More retsina?"

"No, thank you. I've had enough."

"Not as smooth as French wine, is it?" Sotoris asked, grinning.

"One has to acquire a tolerance for the turpentine," Phillipa said with a wry smile.

The time to leave arrived at last, and she breathed a little easier. Mission accomplished. At the door, as Giles draped Phillipa's black lace shawl around her shoulders, Sophie said in a puzzled voice, "I thought you told me Robert lost his little finger in an accident, Phillipa."

"That was my older brother, Guy," Phillipa put in quickly, glancing at Giles's neutral expression.

He smiled disarmingly and held up his hands. "Despite all the physical work I did at Rothingham, I have all my digits."

Once inside the BMW, he said tersely, "It seems you and I need to have a conference."

"How can I remember what I may have told someone five years ago?" she snapped.

"I hope you will remember everything, starting with the day you were born. We are not going to take any more chances of blowing our operation."

Her hands clutched the steering wheel. On the hill ahead of her, in Old Town, spotlights lit up the Acropolis, where medieval mercenaries had clanked about in armor. "Well, let's see," she said tartly. "When I was six weeks old, I remember seeing something bright red, except I didn't know then that was the name of the color."

"We're not playing games, Lady Phillipa. We're talking about discovering a traitor who is plotting to betray the Macedonian government—and doubtless assassinate your precious Damon in the process."

"He is not my precious Damon," she said in a quiet, controlled tone.

"No, he is Sigourney's precious Damon, and you would be wise to forget him."

In the darkness of the car her voice was a whisper, filled with a sadness she hadn't meant to exhibit. "You've never been in love, have you?"

"I'm engaged to a young Welsh woman. Will that qualify?"

She ignored the humor in his tone. "Being engaged is not necessarily being in love."

"Love? That furious excitement that pounds through your blood when you're with the person of your dreams? Not really, though I probably could have let myself fall in love with Khalid's new wife, the beautiful Alyx."

"Let yourself? That's not love. Not if you can stop yourself. Love is . . ."

"What?" he jeered softly.

"Love is laughter and tears, rejoicing and grieving. It's suffering through bad breath in the morning, ignoring the first signs of baldness and overlooking pregnancy's stretch marks. It's—"

"You've had a child?"

"Aaron and I lost our only child. Stillborn."

"You feel these...*symptoms*...of love for Damon?"

"I never told you I loved him. That is your own erroneous conclusion."

"I doubt it, Lady Phillipa. I seldom misjudge human nature. Now, tell me about your childhood."

If only his eloquent Welsh voice wasn't so damned seductive, made more so by the darkened intimacy of the car. "All right, I give in. Guy was seven when I was born."

"Where?"

"You *are* thorough, aren't you?" She sighed and said, "At Rothingham Manor. When I was eleven, Robert was born. My brothers and I love the old place. When Guy inherited the estate he also inherited eight hundred pounds and a heap of problems, along with woodworm and the deathwatch beetle. But he has stoutly maintained that one has a moral duty to keep the estate going."

"Tell me about your family," he said—rather peremptorily, she thought, and she had to wonder if her personal aside had bored him.

"My father's title carried a seat in the House of Lords, but he found the minutiae of politics tedious. In the Borders region of Rothingham a kind of feudal system remains intact. The castle, for example, dominates the town in more ways than one. My father was occupied night and day with merely running the family estate, and in that capacity he employed quite a few of the town's residents—approximately 250. But you're probably already familiar with the sort of life-style I'm talking about.''

''Hardly. My father, then eventually I myself, inherited the worthless title of baronet and lands that were taxed beyond keeping. Somehow we did keep Cambria, though. My mother hired out to do laundry. My three brothers, my father and I worked the coal mines. Accidents and the black lung killed them.''

''I'm sorry.''

He laughed shortly. ''Don't be. Even the rich don't escape death. Had I been a wealthy baronet, I might not have been challenged to go beyond my tidy borders. As it was, I earned a scholarship to put me through college and there I watched and studied those students of distinguished lineage and abundant wealth.

''Know what I gleaned from my observations?'' he asked in a dry, sardonic voice. ''That the poor and middle class speak very fast, with quick movements, to attract attention. The rich and powerful—take bonnie Prince Charlie walking with his arms behind his back—move slowly and speak slowly. They don't need to get attention, because they already have it.

''Now tell me about your childhood, your brothers, especially Robert,'' he said, easily switching subjects, as if he had said more than he'd intended. ''I want to know every childhood scrape, any operations, all awards, his interests, whatever.''

"For a mere baronet, you really are autocratic.''

"How forgetful of me. I should remember that your family earldom outranks my baronetcy.''

"Don't be snide." She turned the BMW into the winding, oak-lined drive leading toward Mercuros. Welcoming lights glimmered from the villa's multitude of windows. "I'm tired and want to go to bed. We will discuss my family tree at a later time.''

No sooner was she out of the car than he caught up with her on the graveled drive. His hand clamped over her upper arm. "No," he said in a coolly polite tone, "we will discuss it now. Tonight.''

Silly, how the touch of this man—a mere mercenary—could set her off, weaken her resolve. Above them, a sliver of a moon hung mysteriously in the heavens, like a new bride, waiting. She shook her head, as if by doing so she could shake off her feminine weakness, and drew a deep, steadying breath. "Really, Giles," she said, "you're being rather ridiculous about all this.''

"My name is Robert," he warned in a low whisper. "Your beloved brother, remember? The servants have ears, sis." His hand slipped down her bare arm, rubbing it in a warning gesture that shook her to the bone. How much longer could she continue this charade? "You're chilled, Phillipa. Let's go inside.''

Daphne opened the door for them and announced in her loud voice, "You have a visitor, my lady, waiting in the sitting room."

Hands behind his back, a hulk of a man dressed totally in black perused the arrangement of framed photographs mounted on one wall of the sitting room. Several of the photographs were of a towheaded Robert as a child. The tawny-haired Giles could pass tolerably well as her younger brother.

At their entry the massive old man turned and said heartily, "Phillipa, my child!" The intelligent rheumy eyes in the sunken sockets moved past her to the man whose hand clasped her shoulder protectively. "Sir Robert Bowmont, isn't it? So you accepted Damon's challenging proposition as director of reconstruction projects, I believe?"

"Father Murphy. Well, I'll be damned."

"I sincerely hope not, my son." He glanced back to Phillipa. "You don't perchance have any wine to offer—consecrated, of course."

She smiled and shut the double doors behind her for privacy. "And if I don't? Will a glass of Taittinger suffice?"

"Alas," he said, plopping his bulk into a nearby armchair, "I shall have to do penance, but I wager the potent brew shall be worth it."

Giles arched a golden brow in amusement. "A priest who drinks. What would the church say?"

"'I drink to make other people more interesting.' That's by George Nathan."

Chuckling to herself, she crossed to a sideboard and filled three tulip glasses. She handed one glass to Father Murphy and another to Giles. In some unidentifiable way Giles reminded her not only of Damon, but of that charismatic Arab, Khalid, who was also accustomed to getting what he wanted and a supreme male chauvinist, unless his recent marriage to his Alyx had changed him.

Father Murphy was saying, "Damon has charged me with assisting you in any way I can, my son."

Giles turned his glass between his fingers, staring at its sun-golden liquid. "How do I know I can trust even you, Father?"

Within the rubbery folds of his face Father Murphy's amiable grin appeared. "What? You impugn my ecclesiastical calling?" He winked and added more somberly, "On the other hand, you actually have no choice, do you, my son?"

"I'll vouch for Father Murphy," Phillipa said. "Then I'll leave you two to hatch your nefarious plots while I seek the sleep of the innocent."

As she climbed the stairs she caught fragmented sentences. "...every office of the National Palace...the confessional is sacrosanct!...wiretapped..."

A hot bath in her antique tub with lions-claw feet did nothing to diminish the unidentifiable yearning that had flowered while she'd watched the shared glances and nonverbal communication between Sophie and Sotoris. Damon and Sigourney shared that same intense emotional and spiritual communication. If only she, too, could know that feeling.

Phillipa wanted to cry out at the injustice of life. Aaron, a professor of archaeology, had been fifteen years older than she, and their marriage had been one of quiet, steady affection and admiration. She had never really bought the image pushed by romantic films and novels that there was more to love than that.

After meeting Damon she had realized how utterly, foolishly, naively blind she had been. When she had first seen him her heart had galloped like a racehorse, her throat had gone dry, and her stomach had sunk like a lead weight all the way to her toes.

No, she would never know the wild, drenching passion that was Sigourney's. But then, Sigourney was world-famous and beautiful. And young.

Toweling her slight body dry, Phillipa could not help but grimace at her reflection in the bedroom's full-length mirror. You are most fortunate to have a veneer of culture and polish to conceal how unprepossessing you are, Lady Phillipa Fleming, she told herself.

Suddenly, behind her reflection, she saw the startled Giles framed in the bedroom doorway, and she spun around. Unaccustomed to having a man in the house, she had left the door open. She clutched the towel in front of her. Her throat and tongue refused to work, but at last she got out, "What . . . what do you want?"

He simply stared at her. A muscle twitched in his jaw. She was too stunned by the blatant desire she saw in his eyes to say anything else. Involuntarily her body responded to his smoldering look. Her nipples budded tautly against the towel's high pile, and heat blossomed between her thighs.

For the first time she realized that her quick incisive mind, her intellect, which she had always been able to rely on, was just a small part of her being, a precarious minority ruling over the emotional mass that made up the remainder of her.

He loosened his tie, and she was half afraid and half hopeful—of what, she wasn't certain. She was wild with curiosity, with fear, a fear that she was sure he could see trembling on her lips, quenching her social smile, forcing her to lower her eyes, stiffening her posture so that she would not shake.

"I stopped by," he said, "to tell you that I invited Father Murphy to breakfast tomorrow morning so we could finish our discussion."

Such banal words. She could only nod.

The slightest semblance of a smile tugged at his youthful mouth. "Your derriere is delightful, Phillipa."

She whirled, realizing that her exposed backside had been reflected in the mirror, and unintentionally presented him with a view of the authentic thing. She spun around again, feeling the scarlet heat rise from her toenails all the way up to her lips.

"Good night, sis." His expression was a perfect poker face.

After he left a secret shame badgered her as she slipped into a rose silk sleep teddy. My God, Phillipa,

he's fourteen years younger than you! The demoraliz-
ing knowledge did not decrease the longing reflower-
ing, after a long, long time of agonizing loneliness.

At her age... What in God's name was wrong with
her?

Chapter 3

Phillipa hesitated at the closed bedroom door. For the
second time she knocked. When Giles didn't answer
she turned the knob and opened the door several inches
to peek in. Surprisingly, the lamp on the large rose-
wood desk was still lit, even though the early morning's faint light spilled through the window's gauzy
curtains. Scattered across the desk were papers deal-
ing with Macedonia's new hydroelectric project, on
which Giles had started work.

He had fallen asleep with the light still burning. For
the past week he had been running himself ragged with
this ridiculous masquerade, playing catch-up day and
night with Macedonia's lagging governmental projects
and simultaneously working as an undercover agent for
the Pan-Hellenic Free Forces. She saw the effects of his

double life in his shadowed eyes and curt replies to her, though when he was with others he didn't let his congenial Englishman's mask slip.

She hated to awaken him, but Father Murphy was waiting below, drinking a glass of orange juice. She crossed to the wide bed and halted abruptly. A sleeping Adonis lay there, and the overpowering maleness of him hit her like a blow. Even though he slept, she could sense his power and his willfulness. His limbs were tangled in the covers; his skin, tanned darkly by his years in the desert with Khalid, was a gleaming contrast to the white sheets.

She was dumbstruck by his masculine beauty. Her breath was taken away by a sudden primal longing. Her bemusement lasted perhaps only two or three moments; but then, so did an earthquake, which her bemusement could just as well have been, she thought bitterly, judging by the damage it had done to her ordered life.

Hesitantly she reached out and touched his shoulder, so broad against her small hand, and so muscular. Quickly she withdrew her hand. "Giles . . . Giles, wake up."

Instantly his eyes opened, alert and piercingly blue. He sat upright, and the rumpled sheet slipped off to reveal the unmistakable evidence of his masculinity.

Immediately she turned away. "It's Father Murphy. He's down below, waiting for you."

His hand captured hers, and at his touch she went both physically and mentally taut. Her hand curled into a tight ball. "Sorry," he said. "It's all right. I'm covered now."

Without glancing at him, she slipped her hand from his grasp. "I'll tell Father Murphy you'll be down."

Oh, Phillipa, she demanded of herself, how could you act so gauche? You're no spinster. You've seen a naked man before. Pull yourself together!

Nevertheless, when she joined the old priest in the sunny breakfast nook, she was definitely rattled. "Giles... er, Robert... will be down shortly, Father." She glanced around to see if anyone was within hearing. Another slipup like that and Giles's cover could be blown.

Father Murphy's shaggy white brows beetled down with concern over his intelligent eyes. He laid his butter knife on the plate's edge. "Are you feeling well, my daughter? You're very pale."

"I'm fine, Father, really. I just need my coffee first thing in the morning in order to get oriented for the rest of the day." She willed her hand not to shake as she poured herself a cup of the thick, syrupy Turkish liquid. "Are you certain you won't have an American breakfast, Father—eggs, bacon, toast, all the trimmings?"

He swallowed a bite of the warm, home-baked sesame seed loaf and said, "This *koulouria* is more than enough. Delicious!" He patted his rotund girth. "Although why I try to diet, I don't know. The best way to lose weight, I've found, is to get the flu, then take a trip to Egypt."

She chuckled, and some of the tension eased from her features. The ugly old priest always seemed to put things in perspective for her. Surely she had blown the moment at Giles's bedside out of proportion.

"We are alone, my daughter?" Father Murphy asked in a hushed voice.

"Yes. Daphne is upstairs with the chambermaid, going over the morning's chores, and the cook is in the kitchen, having her breakfast. I left word that we were not to be disturbed unless I rang."

"Good. When Giles joins us, we need to discuss what we are—"

"Morning, Father. Phillipa."

Phillipa's head turned. For once Giles was dressed casually, though quite fashionably. She recognized his cotton twill bushman's shirt and safari loafers as expensive men's boutique items, but his jeans were old, faded and washed enough to mold his hardened thighs. Her gaze swerved back to her coffee. She could feel herself blushing.

"Burning your candle at both ends are you, my son? Sorry to waken you so early, but Damon wanted me to pass along some news to you."

Giles slid into the chair opposite Phillipa, and she asked him, "Coffee?"

"From the glum look on Father Murphy's face, I think I'm going to need it."

"Alas, my old face always looks this bad. But down to business." He hunched over the wrought-iron table as far as his girth would allow. "Early this morning, before dawn, our main military installation in the Alexandros Valley was bombed.''

Giles took the cup she passed him. "What kind of damage was sustained?"

His rich Welsh voice was calm, his cool features unruffled, his blue eyes sleepy and at half mast, his body relaxed in the chair, but she knew that his trenchant mind was already calculating with a rapid, computer-like efficiency all the variables of what he knew so far about Alexandros.

"Only the communications satellite and cypher-intelligence sections were hit. It appears to have been one of those homemade bombs. No one was hurt, fortunately. And no one seems to know how the terrorist entered the compound. It's better guarded than Fort Knox."

"Unless it was an inside job," Giles mused.

"But why those sections?" Phillipa asked him. "Why not more important areas—tanks, armaments, things like that?"

"Any number of reasons. Damon had turned over to the cypher-intelligence section an anonymous letter addressed to him. That's hardly sufficient cause in itself, but then again, maybe the bombing was just a warning of sorts—demonstrating to the Macedonian people the strength of the Pan-Hellenic Free Force's opponents."

"Have you given any thought to the possibility that the PFF's unseen enemy might not be just the MPA, but also the New Democracy Party?" Father Murphy asked. "They were Agamemnon's legal political opponents until PFF overthrew him."

She ignored the old priest's question and asked anxiously, "What did the letter contain?" Had Damon's life been threatened?

Giles appraised her coolly. "A threat. He was told to call off the Midsummer Midnight festivities." He turned his attention back to Father Murphy. "The New Democracy Party's involvement *is* a possibility. Who's in charge of the communications and intelligence section?"

"A woman by the name of Melina Simonpetra," Father Murphy said.

"Melina's been with the Pan-Hellenic Forces since Damon recruited her six or seven years ago," she elaborated for Giles.

"Perhaps I should get to know Melina better," Giles said, and took a swallow of his coffee. "I think you should throw a welcoming party for your brother," he said to her. "Invite all your friends and associates."

"I don't think that's a good idea," she snapped, irritated at his authoritative command. This was, after all, *her* home. Her one retreat from the pressure of her own double life.

"Why not?" he asked, his unreadable expression never altering.

Purposefully she replied with a patronizing smile guaranteed to set the most vehement chauvinist's teeth on edge. She was fighting her unnatural attraction to him with all her feminine wiles. "Because inviting

Macedonia's cabinet would automatically align me with them politically. As it is, I have managed to appear apolitical."

He didn't take the bait, but reminded her equably, "That was until your brother went to work for them. As it is, it's entirely logical that you would want to show off your younger brother to anyone and everyone. Invite members of the New Democracy Party, as well as Macedonia's illustrious socialites. That way you appear to be impartial, and I have a good chance to assess any potential traitors in our midst."

He was persistent. She sighed and said, "Very well. Have it your way."

Giles calculated the social weight of the guests in Phillipa's villa. A veritable gold mine. Phillipa entertained discreetly, but lavishly. Phillipa—queenly, silk-clad Phillipa.

Watching her converse with her multitude of guests, subtly maneuvering individuals from group to group, Giles thought that he had known housemaids and debutantes, and both patterned themselves after an ideal. The ideal was Phillipa. She had a quality of consummate rarity, and a quiet beauty that crept up on the unsuspecting. Each detail of her face was perfection, yet the whole was simple, as only the purest beauty could be.

She had the uncompromising eyes of a child, and this worried him. Was she out to prove that she was more than just one of those Limousine Liberals? And, if so, what was she? Was she a member of the leftist terrorist group? He sensed that with this woman he needed to keep all his wits about him.

Amid the clinking of lead crystal glasses and the light social chatter and sparkling laughter, he observed her moving around the crowded room, making each guest feel at ease. He thought that she seemed as fragile as a hothouse flower transplanted into unsuitable soil, and yet how tenacious she was. From what Father Murphy had intimated, he knew she never gave up, never allowed herself to fail.

Although she was petite, barely over five foot two, she looked statuesque, undeniably female. Gwynfor and the other women he had known had skin that was firm, but tough from sun worshipping, buttocks that were rounded but too muscular, and breasts that were childlike and unformed. But the ivory-skinned Phillipa possessed a soft, ripe womanliness, with gently swaying breasts that inflamed him.

She was a grown woman, with a grown woman's experience; an aristocrat of distinguished lineage; a freedom fighter of uncommon courage; and an undercover agent—of possibly questionable loyalties.

Just watching her talking with one of the guests, Giles remembered the sight of her naked in her bedroom mirror, and he felt afire. His head was hammering. The blood was rushing through his body like an express train so that he tingled all over.

It was obvious to him that she was in love with the man who was talking with her. Not just any man, but

Macedonia's brilliant, selfless leader: Damon Demetrios.

A tinge of jealousy, a first for him, needled his ego. But overriding the jealousy was real concern that she was the one responsible for the sabotage of Damon's administration. *A woman scorned*...

Reluctantly, he began to wend his way through the crush of guests to the hallway. With the party in full swing, both she and her staff would be occupied below, and his temporary absence would go unnoticed.

He had gotten only as far as the double doors when a young woman wearing a no-nonsense white flight suit stepped boldly in front of him. His trained powers of observation swiftly took in the angular face, the carmine lips and the flat cheekbones below flashing Gypsy-black eyes.

Here was a streetwise creature, he thought, who didn't know the meaning of fear. He doubted whether the woman, who couldn't be more than twenty-four or five, had completed a higher education, but he wasn't so unwise as to dismiss her as ignorant. He would have bet his secret service pension that this young woman was as shrewd as they came.

She pushed her straight dark brown hair, severely but flatteringly cut just below her square jawline, behind one ear, which was spangled with a gold hoop earring, and smiled broadly. "Lieutenant Melina Simonpetra. And you are the honorable Sir Robert Bowmont, no?"

He had been meaning to get around to her that evening, and he supposed now was as good a time as any.

Over her head, he saw Phillipa dart a glance at him, but it appeared to him that she couldn't bring herself to meet his gaze. "Robby will do just fine," he told the young Greek warrior-woman before him.

He took her elbow and drew her into the highly polished, empty marble hallway. Hand braced beside her head on the wall, he stared down into her blatantly hungry eyes. Her nostrils flared, and he caught the hot scent of desire emanating from her. With a woman like this, he didn't mince words. He wasn't fooled by her interest in him. No doubt he reminded her of Damon. Father Murphy had pointed out their similarities the night he had stayed late. Was every woman in Macedonia in love with the country's leader?

He whispered harshly, "I've been watching you all night." Which was true—at least partially—but not for the reason she probably surmised.

Her fingers crept out to loosen the knot of his bluestriped Hermes tie. "You look like a caged animal, Robby."

"I was aroused the whole time you were talking so politely in there."

That was true, too. But it was soft, womanly Phillipa, with her lovely, heart-shaped face, who had triggered such a powerful sexual longing in him. She was the original Eve, he thought. This morning he had awakened from his dreams of her, hard and hurting, only to find her there, within touching distance. The urge to grab her, pull her down under him on the bed, to thrust himself on her and in her and batter down her cool, contained wall had almost been stronger than his self-control. Such behavior was that of a young man in the first hot lust of independence. Where was the discipline he had fought so hard to attain?

Melina pressed her hips against him and her eyes gleamed with anticipation. He almost grinned, thinking of the kick she would have deftly delivered to his unprotected masculinity had she discovered the inspiration for his arousal. He had the distinct feeling this proud young woman would stomp a hole in him without a second thought if she knew what was going on in his mind.

Her tongue darted out to lick her glistening lips, reminding him of a kitten eager to play. She was so young still, not realizing that the greatest sexual satisfaction came from a mutual meeting of the mind and soul, and that that precious condition occurred only very rarely between two individuals. "Can you get away from your watchful sister tonight?" she asked him outright.

He chuckled softly, and slowly caressed the strong column of her neck. Beneath his fingers he felt her tremble of excitement. "From a party in my honor? I doubt it seriously. My sister would have my head served on the breakfast tray tomorrow morning."

"I didn't plan to let her have you back until tomorrow night."

"In time for the dinner tray? Thanks, but I have a better idea. Why don't I drop by to see you tomorrow? You work at the Alexandros installation, don't you?"

Her lips parted in expectation. "I'd like that. I'll arrange for a visitor's permit to be left at the main gate."

"Good. Now go on back in there. I'll join you in a few minutes."

Her full lips thrust out in a pretended pout, but her gaze was totally direct and honest. She wouldn't be one to play games; he liked that about her.

Once she was gone he took the wide steps at the end of the hallway two at a time. First he tried Phillipa's office. The door was unlocked, which meant he probably would find nothing of importance there. Nevertheless, he gave her desk a thorough search, looking both inside her desk drawers and under and behind them for false bottoms. Next he went through her cabinets, seeking anything of a suspicious nature—a listening device, tape recorder or stored private files. When even the prismed light fixture and the lined velvet drapes failed to yield anything, he abandoned the office and, checking the hallway for wandering guests, headed for her bedroom.

The expensive jade lamp in her Oriental-style bedroom was lit, and he made a quick sweep of her closet shelves and dresser drawers. He doubted he would find any incriminating evidence there. Privately he was hoping he wouldn't stumble on any incriminating evidence anywhere. He really didn't like the nasty little aspects of his job—the snooping and lying and invasion of other people's most private lives.

An informant with the Irish Republican Army had once told him that an undercover operative's job was tantamount to mental rape. The seedy image the snitch had painted gave Giles an unpleasant sensation at the back of his throat. One day soon he hoped to get out of this line of work before he was permanently tainted, unable to distinguish the line that divided right and wrong.

The bedroom light spilled over into the bathroom, with its hand-painted porcelain fixtures. There he literally stumbled on a mound of lingerie discarded next to a malachite Jacuzzi. He picked up the garment on top, a pair of panties. Without realizing what he was doing, he fingered the lacy, lilac garment, lifting it and crushing it against his jaw. Soft and satiny and scented with Phillipa's personal sachet and, even more subtly, her own glorious woman's scent.

Dismayed by his weakness for this fascinating woman, he dropped the panties exactly where they had been and felt along the wall for the light switch. He needed light, if only to allay his old fear of the dark— that mind-numbing phobia left over from the coal mining days of his childhood.

"What are you doing in here?"

His head jerked around. Phillipa stood behind him, taut as a startled woodland animal. The room's plush, deep-pile carpet must have silenced her approach.

Never make explanations was his philosophy, and he didn't. As he did on a rugby field, he took the offense and pulled her stiff, resisting body into his arms. God, her small, soft feminine shape felt so good! She stared

rebelliously up at him, the proud curve of her cheek
caught in the dim light from the bedroom.

He bent his head and kissed her tightly compressed
mouth. "Open your mouth, Phillipa," he said against
the lips that trembled beneath his.

He felt her fists thud once against his chest; then her
hands splayed over his dinner jacket, and her lips went
pliant, parting for his thrusting tongue. Desire swept
through him with the force of an island hurricane, and,
like an island, he was unprepared for its fierceness. He
had the bewildering sensation of unknown horizons
opening up before him.

Could she feel him throbbing with his unconcealed
passion for her? Her small tongue hesitantly con-
nected with his, and he thought he might explode then
and there. When his hand brushed her breast she
groaned, and he knew with a man's sure instinct that
she was as ready as he, that if he backed her against the
wall, standing up, he could take both of them over the
edge in seconds.

"Phillipa, darling? Where did you go?"

At the sound of Sigourney's voice he released Phillipa at once. Both of them were breathing heavily.
"Don't ever do that again," she whispered hoarsely.

She spun from him and hurried into the outer room.
"I didn't find a safety pin, Sigourney," she called in a
deceptively sedate voice, "but I'm certain Daphne will
know where she stored the sewing kit."

For the rest of the evening he observed Phillipa as
she moved through the roomful of guests, successfully

maintaining her serenity by avoiding eye contact with him. He hurt more than ever with his wanting of her. Was she hot under her gown with her own wanting?

With rueful astonishment he realized that for once in his life he was getting in over his head. Apparently he had spent far too many years in the Arabian deserts, leading a life devoid of emotion, if not of sexual liaisons with the willing bedouin girls and aristocratic Arab women, bored by the semisequestered lives imposed on them. He remembered watching Arab princesses cruise the desert roads in their limousines to look over and pick up strange men, all for a single night's passionate encounter, strictly forbidden, on pain of execution.

And here he was, becoming involved with a woman who might possibly be a double agent, beguiled by a woman who he suspected was in love with another man, while he himself had a fiancée waiting back in Wales.

An affair—not a passing sexual conquest, but an affair that involved his total emotional makeup, especially an affair with an older woman, a woman of Phillipa's caliber—would endanger the very quality that made him so successful at his work: his by-now legendary detachment.

He'd better get this mission over with and get out while he still had some control over his emotions.

Chapter 4

She was on a sexual collision course with a man four-teen years younger!

Uneasily Phillipa steered her BMW out toward the highway leading to the valley of Alexandros and Macedonia's main military installation. The drive should have been a pleasant one. Summer's lavender flowers filled the passing fields, and lambs cavorted in the brilliant green pastures. She was reminded of the region surrounding Rothingham, where most of the golden stone houses with their thatched roofs were older than some countries.

She slid a surreptitious glance at the handsome but stern profile of the man sitting beside her. In the intimate confines of the automobile his masculinity was more potent than ever. And dangerous. She would be glad when he was given his governmental car.

That morning Giles had been the essence of propriety. It was, she thought, as if last night had never happened, as if he had never kissed her. Perhaps he regretted it. She certainly did.

Ignorance *is* bliss, she thought somewhat bitterly.

She breathed shallowly, remembering acutely that kiss, the voyage of his tongue, how his fingers, just barely brushing her breast, had triggered spasms that had left her stunned.

Anxiously she wondered if it were possible for her to grow addicted to such satisfaction. The mere act of crossing her legs later in the evening had sent short jolts of arousal through her and left her dying for more of his touch during the rest of the evening.

She valued her dignity. She had earned it. Anyone who reached middle age deserved a certain respect for her accumulation of life's scars. And she hated the thought of throwing away that dignity and the respect she valued, all that were left to her in what modern psychoanalysts pooh-poohed as the middle-age crazies.

Memories flooded through her, memories of Aaron and the university and overhearing a cocky male student brag about bedding the wife of one of the professors. "I tell you, those older women are grateful."

Recalling the young man's boast, she cringed with shame—and, yes, anger. Never would she submit to such a degrading situation.

Giles asked, "Are you all right?"

Those were the first words they had exchanged since setting out. For the fourth straight morning he had left his light burning, she had noticed, although she would have sworn he hadn't brought papers home to work on last night, because of the party.

"Yes, I'm fine." She unbuttoned the black-and-white jacket she wore over her sundress. She was flushed and perspiring, and it wasn't from the mid-morning heat.

Keep the conversation light, she told herself. "I'm curious why we're checking out the Alexandros military installation when Damon could easily have arranged a complete tour for you."

"Because then everything would have been in perfect order. No, I think the casual approach is better."

A steep curve lay just ahead, and she downshifted. "Does Melina know I'm coming along?"

Giles grinned, something he rarely did. The effect of that smile hit her with the force of a nuclear meltdown. "I felt it would be better to give her a pleasant surprise." His hand, tanned and strong with youth, rested lightly on one thigh. That morning he looked so crisp, so fresh, in white slacks and a white raw silk shirt and navy blue blazer.

Two small vertical lines creased the bridge of her nose. "So I'm to be a diversion?"

He laid his hand over hers, where it held the gearshift, and she inhaled sharply, tingling all over at his touch. "Phillipa... about last night. I am—"

"Please. Don't say anything, Giles. You're engaged and I'm . . . I'm involved with someone."

"Of course," he said after a moment, apparently accepting her lie.

Did he think the man with whom she was involved was Damon? she wondered. If so, then he had to think less of her. Oh, what a tangled web we weave . . .

He removed his hand. "I acted like an ass, and I would like to apologize. I suppose I must have had too much to drink."

Somehow she had to salvage what was left of her pride. "Living in close quarters as we do, sharing the dangers involved with undercover work . . . What happened was naturally understandable. It just must not happen again, Giles. Something like that . . . Well, it would surface somehow. Soon it would become apparent to everyone that we aren't brother and sister, and that could jeopardize the whole operation."

The strong lines of his mouth compressed with a look of self-disgust that wounded her. The ignominious situation was an embarrassment for both of them. "Naturally you're right."

The ensuing silence was a strain, and she broke the tension by asking, "How long were you with the British Secret Service, Giles?"

"Too long," he told her, with a conspiratorial half smile.

She almost sighed with relief. He was teaming with her to keep their relationship platonic. In the days and weeks to come she was not going to have to worry about giving herself away, about betraying her supreme fascination for this man who was so much younger than herself.

"I worked for MI6 for a year, and M11 for six months," Giles was saying. "Just long enough to learn evasive driving, surveillance, unarmed combat, field craft, training in weapons—those sorts of things."

"Why did you leave the Secret Service? I imagine you would be the perfect candidate—intelligent, single, an adventurer."

"I wounded my left knee in a fracas. Not badly. But it's somewhat insubordinate—cosmetically sound, but gimpy." He chuckled. "I was told to get out or I'd have one very straight leg."

She smiled. "In Toridallos, I met a woman whose leg had been..." Another slipup. She was getting frightfully lax. No one, not even Damon, knew the full story of those horrible days there.

"Toridallos?"

"A prison."

"Yes, I've heard of it. Its infamy is well-known, even as far as Baghrashi. And for something to be infamous in Baghrashi, I assure you it has to top the charts. So you were in that hellhole."

His casual acceptance of the fact, no pitying glances, no curious questions, put her at ease with that part of her past for the first time. Not even Father Murphy's gentle concern had achieved that.

"Thirty-one days. Seven-hundred and fifty hours of solitary confinement, more or less. You can't help but come face-to-face with yourself—and, if you're lucky, you come to terms with yourself."

"Did you?"

She chewed on her bottom lip, wanting badly to free herself of the nightmares of being grilled by the agents of VASIK, an acronym for Agamemnon's Gestapo-like security police. But she knew instinctively that sharing such a terribly private thing would weaken her defenses against Giles, against his strength, charm and youth.

She settled for a simple reply. "I learned in Toridallos that the nobility of mankind is no cliché, that it does exist."

"How did you arrive at that conclusion?"

She heard the cynicism edging his voice. "You don't hold the same belief?"

"I have yet to witness the nobility of mankind."

She thought about Father Murphy and Mother Teresa and all the other beautiful souls in the world who truly practiced the biblical command to love one another. "In Toridallos I had to clean my cell once a week by sweeping the dirt through a small square opening at the bottom of my cell door. Later a trustee-inmate would collect the dirt, along with that from the other cells, and sweep it down the long center hall.

"After the first three weeks—only three weeks, mind you—of going without seeing or speaking to another individual, I was hungry for human warmth and kindness. One day the trustee put her hand through the hole and I grabbed it. Just the touch of another's skin... I wept like a baby over her hand. And she was humane enough to squeeze my hand before she had to withdraw her own. That one small gesture gave me enough support, fortitude, or whatever you want to call it, to withstand everything else.''

A muscled flickered in Giles's jaw. He looked away from her, staring out at the countryside. ''You are quite an amazing lady, Phillipa,'' he merely said, as if it were only a passing comment.

She said nothing, grateful that he had listened, but pried no further.

Just ahead was Melpomene, an ancient marketplace that overlooked the valley of Alexandros and Macedonia's main military installation: a maze of variously sized buildings; formidable watchtowers; tarpaper black barracks; and vast training grounds, all surrounded by twelve-foot-high barbed-wire fences. Here, military history abounded. This area of Macedonia had been ruled by the powerful military state of Sparta.

Smartly uniformed in dark blue, the guard on duty at the main checkpoint glanced at his pass list, stepped inside the small brick-and-glass enclosure to place a call, then returned to tell her and Giles, briskly but politely, ''Lieutenant Simonpetra will be with you in just a few minutes. You may park over there while you are waiting.''

''What do you expect to find?'' Phillipa asked Giles after she had parked the car. He had half turned, draping his arm across the back of her seat, and she was uncomfortably aware of him, of the way his masculine presence filled the car, overwhelming her.

"Maybe you can tell me that."

Her gaze swerved to his face. The hard male vitality of his features was stamped with a ruthlessness that took her by surprise. "What do you mean?" For a long moment she braved the rapier thrust of his gaze, pinned where she sat.

Then, startling her, he leaned forward with calm deliberation and kissed her temple, where wisps of her hair curled. "Nothing. Forget what I said. It wasn't that important, anyway." His voice was muffled by her hair, his anger seemingly directed at himself.

Her lashes fluttered down. The intimacy of the car made it too easy to overlook their age differences. With almost treacherous persistence her heartbeat hammered in her eardrums. "I don't believe you, Giles. Whatever you said was import—"

Drawing away from her, he said in a warning tone, "She's here—Melina."

Apprehensively she glanced over her shoulder and saw the guard pointing out her car to Melina. She hoped that the woman hadn't spotted them first.

Melina had forgone the usual skirt and jacket assigned to females in the military in favor of tailored khaki trousers and a shirt and tie. Despite the masculine attire, she still exuded a blatant sensuality as she strode toward them. Her thick but well-defined brows lifted at the sight of Phillipa.

Giles got out of the car to greet Melina, and she gave him a quick possessive kiss, then flashed a halfhearted smile through the window at Phillipa. The woman was obviously very much infatuated with Giles. Phillipa felt a twinge of guilt at accompanying him. She truly liked Melina, who was independent, courageous and loyal.

Or at least Phillipa believed her to be loyal.

"Have you ever been on a military post before, Robby?" Melina asked.

"First time."

"First for you, too, Lady Phillipa?"

Melina knew very well that Phillipa had often been to the military training camp secreted on an island in the Aegean Sea, but she was probably unsure of just how much Phillipa's brother knew of Phillipa's past activities for PFF. "It's a first for me, too," Phillipa confirmed lightly.

The tour of the post, taken in a jeep driven by a male subordinate to Melina, took little more than a couple of hours, though Giles found excuses to linger in both Melina's office and in the shells that were the remains of the communications and intelligence buildings.

"Were you on the post when this happened?" he asked as he prowled through the rubble of bricks and twisted steel girders.

"No, I was . . . Some friends and I had driven up to Constantine for a night on the town."

When at last the tour was over and the jeep returned them to Phillipa's car, Melina leaned forward in her seat and kissed Giles fully on the mouth. Naturally, his arms went around her to support her. Phillipa couldn't help wishing that the young female officer would be sent on a three-year tour of duty in the Antarctic.

"Can you come over tomorrow tonight?" Melina asked huskily. "I live up in Melpomene."

"I'll find you," he promised.

It was infantile to be jealous, Phillipa told herself. She had thought she was above that petty emotion. She tried to remind herself that Giles was far too young for her, that, like a lone wolf, he ran alone, and that, unlike Damon, he cared for nothing beyond his immediate needs.

All these reminders could not negate the appeal of the man. An occupation that demanded a clear head and quick reactions under extreme pressure required a man to be cocky as well as courageous.

"Well, did you learn anything?" she asked him in a tight voice as she drove out of the parking lot and turned back onto the main highway.

"A little."

Lips compressed, she made an effort to brush away her resentment that he didn't trust her enough to elaborate more. After all, he worked for Damon and owed her no explanations.

He glanced at his watch. "It's four o'clock. Time for high tea in London. Would you settle for a bitter in the taverna just ahead?"

Smiling in spite of her disgruntlement, Phillipa turned off into the village of Melpomene, dominated by its ancient marketplace. "Bitter? I haven't heard that since my Oxford days."

"You went to Oxford? So did I."

She parked the car before a venerable taverna with high peeling walls. "I attended University College there." Before he could come around to help her, she slid out from behind the wheel.

"I was at Hartford," he said, taking her elbow in a proprietary gesture and guiding her into the taverna's tree-shaded courtyard and over to one of the few unoccupied tables. The rest were taken by laughing, khaki-clad young soldiers or old men in traditional black garb and jauntily angled berets, sharing that day's village gossip. "I read economics and politics."

At his touch she became almost giddy—and angry with herself, with this new weakness. "Philosophy was my major."

A white-aproned waiter took their order. Giles settled for the piney-tasting retsina in place of the desired draft ale, and she asked simply for mineral water. "Is that where you met your husband?" he asked after the waiter had left.

Aaron—a subject to restore some sanity in her suddenly topsy-turvy world. "Aaron was a professor at Merton." Like Giles, she kept to English, assuring them of some privacy from the ears of the other customers. "We had both escaped a torrential rainstorm by ducking into one of those old, smoky pubs, the Turf."

"The Turf!" Giles grinned at some secret reminiscence, and she was at once captivated by the way the corners of his mouth curved. "I hoisted many a toast there myself. I wonder how many times our paths crossed," he mused, "and we weren't aware of it."

"I doubt our paths ever crossed, Giles," she said dryly, taking the glass of mineral water the waiter had set before her. "You were still in prep school when I was accepting my college diploma."

His expression moody, he stared down into his glass, then lifted his head. His eyes, as pale blue as the Afton River in Scotland, bored into hers. "Are you by any chance trying to tell me that you're too old for me?"

She shrank back into the protective leafy shadows an elm cast over their table. "You are direct, aren't you? Yes, I suppose that's exactly what I'm trying to tell you. I *am* much too old for you."

"How old was your husband when you met him?"

"Thirty-five."

"And you? Twenty or so?"

"Nineteen. But I married him. I'm not planning on marrying you."

He raised a brow and grinned. "Just sucking my blood, is that it?"

She had to smile at that, though wryly. "How did you guess the secret of my longevity?" She attempted to dilute the potent danger of the conversation with levity. "Let me tell you one of Father Murphy's many quotes: 'An archaeologist is the best husband a woman can have. The older she gets, the more interested he is in her.' ''

A perfunctory smile crossed his face. How nice it would be, she mused, to be able to instigate a harmless flirtation with him. But she was too much older, too restrained by dignity and propriety.

He surprised her, taking her hand, which lay on the table in a tight little fist, and one by one uncurling her fingers. She fought to control her suddenly rapid breathing. The sensual excitement he could arouse in her astounded her. "I am a modern man, Phillipa. I cannot and will not accept the double standards of—"

"Of what?" she asked sardonically, and withdrew her hand. "Of my generation?"

"Of others," he said harshly. "Why should an older woman be any different than an older man?"

She rose and dropped her wadded napkin on the table. Her voice was low, barely above a whisper. "Because I'm supposed to be your sister. And that is the only relationship we can possibly share."

She left, but he caught up with her outside the taverna and blocked her way, his hands braced against the wall at either side of her head. His half-shuttered blue eyes slid to her heaving breasts. "All right, love. I'll play by the rules I agreed to when I accepted Damon's offer. I'll be your loving brother—" his head bent and his lips brushed her cheekbone "—for now, at least."

She finally dared to glance at his face, but the almost physical possession of his gaze set her pulse pounding with a tom-tom beat. There was no denying it. Lady Phillipa was beguiled for the first time in her life.

Chapter 5

The home was as bland as the man, Giles thought: an unpretentious, whitewashed house jammed up against its neighbors in the old neighborhood.

He flicked closed the high-carbon steel three-inch jimmie on his penknife and tucked it into the inner pocket of his white linen vest. For several seconds he stood just inside the doorway of Major Veranos's living room, his sharp eyes scanning innocuous items: a lamp; a brass ashtray; and, lastly, a a small square, black ceramic planter—the kind that could house a heat sensor, which would pick up a person's body warmth and activate a silent alarm. Macedonia's internal security commander would almost certainly have installed such a system.

So would the Oracle of Delphi.

In this case, were the two one and the same?

If the room had been wired, Giles estimated that he now had less than thirty seconds to locate the switch box and abort the alarm. A sudden surge of adrenaline pumped through his body, as potent as any drug, as potent—and as dangerous—as his feelings for the Lady Phillipa Fleming.

With the sureness of purpose that had become second nature to him, he strode across the tiled floor into the narrow, outdated kitchen. Yes, it was where he had thought—hoped—it would be: a gray metal switch box, high on one wall.

His hands steady, he grasped the two thick wires feeding into the switch box and deftly clamped them with an alligator clip. He immediately began to breathe easier. The current wasn't broken, yet the alarm signal, if there was one, had been terminated.

He surveyed the kitchen, finding the stock of food meager—in keeping with a bachelor's domain. Then he wandered through the rest of the house. Midday sunlight spilling through the windows revealed an immaculate home, well dusted and Spartan in its furnishings, an indication of the major himself, and a recommendation for the position he held.

Satisfied that the house held no further alarms, he began a more detailed, thorough search of its contents. Quickly, but carefully, so as not to disturb anything, he went through the house, randomly opening drawers and doors.

He was looking for anything out of the ordinary. A hall closet disclosed expensive luggage, which was out of keeping with the major's rather temperate image. However, that was certainly no proof in itself of the man's complicity.

In the only bedroom he found a small, thin-legged desk—not the type to conceal highly classified secrets. Since the desk wasn't locked, he really didn't expect it to yield any surprising documents. Nevertheless, he made a minute inspection of the drawers, finding them virtually empty, if he discounted a few scattered pens and pencils, along with an assortment of clean notepads. Neither did he find any false bottoms or concealed compartments.

Before he left the bedroom he dismantled the antediluvian black telephone with the same rapidity and efficiency he had been trained to use when breaking down an Uzi, probably the most feared weapon in the world. After applying a tap, he reassembled the telephone and wiped the instrument free of prints with his blue silk pocket handkerchief.

Then he returned to the living room and, hands on hips, glanced over the small, ascetic room once more. It would seem for the moment that Major Veranos was cleared of suspicion. That left others—Gregorios Zychapoulos for one. Melina Simonpetra for another. Her alibi for the night of the terrorist bombing was weak. This evening he would pay her the visit he had promised.

There still remained the refined and lovely Lady Phillipa Fleming to consider. She was the unlikeliest of candidates for the role of Oracle of Delphi—and, therefore, one of his prime suspects. She was entirely capable of being a double agent. How far did he dare trust her?

He hoped to God she was clean. Not only was he strongly attracted to her, but he really liked her, sincerely liked her. She was very classy, with a certain attitude, a spirit-calming depth of experience and emotion, yet with a blushing shyness so obvious that he felt he could almost see her blood glowing under the porcelain surface of her skin. That vulnerability appealed to him.

Hell, everything about her appealed to him. He was acting like an infatuated schoolboy, eaten up with puppy love. The worst part of it was that he suspected that was exactly how she viewed him, as a smitten schoolboy. But he was a man, and he wanted more than just a schoolboy's exchange of blissful sighs and flirtatious glances. Why was it that when he was around her he felt inexperienced, inarticulate and ridiculously unsure of himself?

In the back of his mind an image was engraved of her hips and buttocks reflected in the mirror, firm, yet of a certain ripeness. Her entire body was like that, mature, but arrested at the perfect point. Thinking of her brought to mind the Osmanthus of China, a flower that blossomed for only a few hours in springtime.

The lovely British aristocrat was reaching her springtime and didn't even know it.

Two hours of driving brought him back to Melpomene, which was home to most of the civilians who worked for the nearby Alexandros military post and their families.

Although it was already eight o'clock, the summer evening was only just now deepening, beginning that mysterious intercourse of the earth's shadows with the sky's lingering light. For him twilight, in its elusiveness, its mutability, its beauty, contained something of the feminine, and also something of the infinite.

Lady Phillipa Fleming was like that, he thought, and then immediately and irritably put the romantic idea out of his mind. He was being paid to be practical, not poetic.

He parked the nondescript gray governmental sedan Damon had finally arranged for in front of Melina's duplex. The house was in one of several blocks of modern homes provided for Alexandros's civilian employees. The community was a model neighborhood of modern duplexes, their lawns a blanket of white gravel that required minimal upkeep.

Melina waited for him at the screen door. Above the sweep of her full Romany cheekbones, her brown eyes glowed with pleasure as she drew him inside. "You had no trouble finding my home?"

"None at all. I merely charmed a secretary in the National Palace records department to let me peek at your personnel file and checked on your address."

He had checked on a lot more than merely her address, but had found little other than the basic personal data.

As she led him toward the kitchen he scanned the small cluttered rooms they passed, storing away details he might need to know later: the location of furniture, doors, windows and so on. The clutter suggested a certain laziness, and her taste was rather eclectic and not at all in keeping with the warrior's image she projected: a slightly worn-looking Danish sofa; a Moorish coffee table; an Early American dining table.

"I prepared something simple for dinner," she said almost shyly, tucking her blunt-cut hair behind her ear, which was bare of jewelry this time. "I wasn't sure just how much you liked Macedonian cuisine."

"You forget my mother was Macedonian." He wasn't going to make the mistake of saying his mother had prepared Macedonian dishes, since Phillipa might once have indicated otherwise to the young woman.

"Could you open this?" she asked, passing him a bottle of cheap Italian wine. At least it wasn't retsina. "While you're doing that, I'll finish setting the table."

He popped the cork and as he filled two wineglasses, watched her move about the U-shaped kitchen.

Melina's skill at cooking surprised him no less than did her decor. She served an outstanding chicken-and-lemon soup she called *avgolemono*, followed by *moussaka*, the national dish of eggplant and lamb. While they ate they joked and talked of inconsequential things, but every so often he inserted camouflaged questions about something important.

Apparently one of his questions wasn't subtle enough, because she stiffened almost imperceptibly as he said, "I really admire the minister of justice, Gregorios Zychapoulos, but I'm having trouble getting to know him. He's rather standoffish, I find. What do you think of him?"

She twirled the stem of her glass between her thumb and forefinger and answered absently, "I don't really know him very well, Robby. Maybe he seems aloof because of other problems."

"What kind of problems?"

"Oh, I don't know." She shrugged. "I hear that his wife is ill, some sort of sclerosis. Problems like that might make someone seems standoffish, something I certainly don't intend to be, Robby."

She wasn't. She set down her glass and reached across the table to take his hand. Wordlessly she pushed back her chair and drew him out of the kitchen and into her bedroom. He was already aroused, undeniably a result of the fact that he had been living in such intimate but frustrated conditions with Phillipa.

In the darkened bedroom Melina folded back the bed's quilted coverlet, then slipped off her clothes and lay down. He, too, discarded his clothing, the last vestige of the difference between civilization and the primal state that lurked in every man. Apparently she wanted none of the preliminary sexual communication between two people that he particularly enjoyed, because she opened her arms and whispered, "I can't wait. Hurry!"

As he moved above her, her body was warm and welcoming, but at the same time solid and somehow unyielding—the opposite of how he suspected Phillipa would be.

Then he went absolutely still, and she whispered, "What is it?"

Suddenly he felt cold. It was the first time it had ever happened to him. Impotence! Astonishment, followed by self-disgust, crawled through him. He levered himself off the bed and stared stonily down at her bewildered face. "It's no use," he lied. "I have a fiancée waiting for me in England."

Enlightenment spread over her Gypsy's dark face. "It's all right," she said, her broad mouth turning up in an easy and reassuring smile. "I understand."

He didn't.

And he cursed Phillipa and her ladylike reticence all the way back to Constantine. Nevertheless, he grudgingly realized how much he cared for her. He knew then that he was going to break off his engagement to Gwynfor as soon as he got back to Wales. She would be angry, since she was looking forward to the prestige that would come with her marriage to him, but not hurt on any emotional level, since she didn't love him—or even know what love was.

Damn Phillipa and Damon and their years of shared experience.

Chapter 6

Perspiration beaded at Phillipa's temples. At least three minutes had passed since she had left the Lazeros bathroom and made her way down the steps into the darkened basement. Her purse-size flashlight swept the musty room, cluttered with dusty packing boxes, a broken rocking horse on its knees and a massive, mosaic icon of St. Nicholas propped against one mudbrick wall.

In a darkened corner she found what Giles had instructed her to look for—the telephone bridge box. The flashlight's quivering beam followed a set of wires from the bridge box to a pocket-size tape recorder lodged behind a concealing cardboard box. With clumsy fingers she extracted the tape and slipped it into her jacket pocket. Her palms were clammy as she inserted a new tape.

Damn. She was no love-galvanized woman like Sigourney, who claimed to be cowardly, yet had almost singlehandedly rescued Damon from the bowels of Toridallos Prison. Nor was she a soldier like Melina. At the thought of the woman Phillipa gritted her teeth.

Late last night, when Giles had finally returned home, she had still been awake, working on Arcadia's account ledgers. He had stopped by her office to tell her curtly, "You need to find a reason to visit Sophie tomorrow and change the tape I planted. We'll meet afterward."

Only after he had finished his instructions and stridden down the hall toward his bedroom had she perceived the reason for his abruptness. The woodsy scent of Melina's perfume, which lingered in her office, told Phillipa of the kind of evening he had passed with the woman.

Her pulses quickened by the fear of discovery, Phillipa hurried up the basement stairs, paused at the door to listen, then, pocketing her flashlight, stepped into the empty hallway.

In the modern chrome kitchen Sophie was kneading dough into a round loaf on the scarred butcher-block counter. Phillipa said, "I was remembering your home on Rhodes, Sophie. It was lovely, but you must enjoy all the modern conveniences this house has."

"You know, Phillipa, it's very nice not to have to go outside to bake my *koulouria*." She paused to punch the dough with a flour-speckled fist. "But, you know, I miss those days...always the ear-deafening thump of Sotoris's chisel and mallet against stone in the outer room...seeing his face at the noonday meal every day...gossiping with our village women. They still preferred the old, modest ways, black scarves and long-sleeved dresses."

She sighed heavily. "Sotoris tells me I must change for the sake of Macedonia. That Macedonia must change. But I am older, set in my ways, not like Melina and those other modern girls with their free-style love and their sights set on married men. Melina had better stop ogling my Sotoris or I will do worse to her than what happened out at the Alexandros Military Post."

At the back of her mind, Phillipa wondered if Sophie could possibly be jealous enough to undermine the very regime for which she had fought.

Sophie nodded in the Greek fashion, moving her head upward, and made a "tss" between her teeth. "I long for the old ways Sotoris and I knew."

"I know what you mean," Phillipa said, tucking the bit of information back in her mind to pull out later. "Since I spent most of my childhood in a rather medieval English village, I yearn for the peacefulness and solitude of Rothingham and Berkshire, rather than the hustle-bustle glamour of modern Constantine and London."

Surely neither Sophie nor Sotoris could possibly be a traitor, Phillipa thought. But then, who within Damon's government was the Oracle of Delphi?

With a sense of disloyalty hanging around her neck like an albatross, Phillipa left the Lazeros home after lunch and went straight to the Main Square. She arrived ten minutes early at the designated sidewalk café. No one wanted to be inside when everybody who was anybody was outside.

Beyond the sidewalk blue-and-white trolleys competed with black taxis for the right-of-way, and motorcycles and bicycles dueled with courageous pedestrians crossing the main boulevard to the marble-arched entrance of the National Gardens.

While she waited for her rendezvous with Giles, she sipped from a cup of the sweet, thick Turkish coffee that could practically hold a spoon upright. When she had returned to Macedonia as an adult she had thought she would never acquire a taste for the eye-opening brew, but drinking it had now become completely natural to her.

As she sipped her coffee and watched the people pass by, it came to her that there was nothing so reassuring as the spectacle of human diversity, the endless parade of others like and unlike oneself.

The golden summer sun shone on her, making her feel like fruit ripening in a market stall. Some of the tension ebbed from her taut muscles. She relaxed and watched the parade of life, feeling almost like a voyeur. Everywhere couples strolled. The swagger of the young, modern Greek males was an optimistic boast. The girls walked with a brisk, supple stride. In the rapt gazes of both sexes there was no false modesty, only an open honesty that proclaimed, "I am attracted to you."

Love pervaded the air, and she found the romantic exchange of glances, hesitant touching and tentative kisses both terribly erotic and slightly depressing. She was aware of time slipping by. Never again would she know that exquisite feeling of a woman in love who was well loved in return.

She felt angry with herself, and a little sorry for herself, too—and horribly afraid. The rest of her life yawned before her frighteningly. As she had often done before, she saw herself in the not too distant future as the stereotyped foolish, aging matron, escorted by a succession of gigolos. But the image rang false. Lonely she might be, but never would she become such an object of ridicule.

A long limo bearing the official seal of Macedonia pulled up to the curb in front of the open café. She watched Giles emerge and walk toward her with his graceful yet totally masculine stride. He wore an elegant gray flannel suit and black oxfords.

"*Bon soir*, sis." He greeted her with a light kiss on her temple and drew out a chair across the tiny table from her.

"Well, if it isn't the Beau Brummell of Macedonia," she joked to cover her ridiculous shyness in his presence.

He flashed an amiable grin. "Someone has to battle the decadence of irresponsible fashion."

All night and all during the day she had been plagued by thoughts of him. How utterly breathtaking he had looked that morning she had come upon him sleeping nude. Smooth and hard as marble, she was certain. Poor Aaron had aged so during their last few years, but she had adored him, anyway. Only a woman was expected to have eternal youth.

A woman had to choose a chair in the shadows, as she had today, so the brutally honest sunlight wouldn't reveal the laughter and age lines life had given her.

Giles signaled to the waiter and ordered a glass of ouzo, the anise liqueur. After the waiter had left she asked, "Where is your governmental car?"

He grimaced, and suddenly he looked very young, very boyish. "It had a flat. Damon insisted I use the official limo." He lowered his voice and asked in English, "You were able to retrieve the tape?"

She nodded and took the lacy handkerchief from her pocket. Within it she had folded the tape. She passed the handkerchief to him. "I don't like spying on my friends, Giles."

In his hard, clean-cut face, his eyes were very solemn. "I wasn't the one who asked you to go through with this operation, remember?"

She lowered her lids. "You're right, of course. The choice was mine."

The waiter returned with Giles's ouzo, and he raised his glass in a toast. *"Yassou."*

With a half smile she lifted her cup and replied, "To your health,.also." She tried to control the nervous quaver in her voice.

Where was the composed Lady Phillipa Fleming who had moved easily in the exclusive circle of royalty? Quickly she took a sip of the lukewarm, syrup-like coffee that remained in the bottom of her cup.

"Did Sophie talk about anything political?"

Phillipa shook her head. "No, not really. She did say something about Melina. For some reason I have the idea she thinks Sotoris is interested in the girl."

"That's an all-too-likely supposition. One hears how middle-age men often lose their sense of proportion and risk everything on a fling with a younger woman— all in a futile attempt to regain their lost youth."

"I think Sophie's suspicion is absurd," she replied tartly, wounded by his acute observation. She should be more careful, she thought, or she would betray to him the symptoms of her own middle-aged insecurities.

He studied her intently over the rim of his glass. "Why do you say that?"

"Because…well, because while Melina may have the morals of an alley cat, she is, at least, open about what she does. I can't see her sneaking around."

It wasn't like her to be catty, and she was immediately overwhelmed by contrition. She blushed and murmured, "Actually Melina, along with every woman in Constantine, has been in love with Damon for years."

"Does that include yourself?"

She looked away from his scrutiny. "I was ... or I thought I was." She glanced back at him, realizing for the first time that Giles's presence had all but driven Damon from her mind. "This is rather personal, isn't it?"

"I yield." He rubbed his clean-shaven jaw. "What you tell me does hold some possibilities. Sophie's jealousy, for one. Selling Macedonian secrets to the MPA could be a way of striking back at a philandering husband. And what about Melina? A rebuff by Damon could be reason enough to trigger her treason. It's altogether possible that either woman would have ample reason for betraying her country."

"That could apply to me, also, couldn't it, Giles? 'Hell hath no fury like a woman scorned,' or something to that effect."

"You and Father Murphy must get on marvelously."

She smiled. "His habit of quoting is infectious."

"He's on my suspect list, as well."

"Father Murphy? Are you out of your mind? That old man is devoted to the Macedonian cause."

"An investigator always considers the most unlikely suspect."

"Sorry," she said shortly, "but I would bet my life against the possibility that Father—"

The screeching tires of a green coupe cut short what she had been about to say. She looked up just in time to see a hand emerge from a broken rear window and hurl an object, which appeared to her to be a tin can.

At that same moment Giles shoved her from her chair and threw himself on top of her. In the next instant a blast thundered against her eardrums, stunning her. For what seemed like an eternity she was aware only of Giles's heavy body covering hers.

From her viewpoint on the pavement she could see some of the patrons struggling to their feet. An old woman had blood matting her gray hair, and a teenage boy seemed to be yelling, but Phillipa couldn't hear him, her ears were ringing so loudly.

She felt Giles shift above her; then he was pulling her to her feet. "Are you all right?" he asked, his eyes searching her face intently.

She nodded, reading his lips more than hearing his voice. Dazed, she looked around her at the debris. Most of the patrons appeared to have superficial wounds from flying glass. With the shock wearing off, she realized what she had witnessed: terrorists hurling an incendiary bomb at the sidewalk café.

Fortunately it appeared as though the bomb had been inaccurately thrown, sailing through the café's expansive plate-glass window, with the near-empty interior taking the brunt of the explosion.

Giles was pulling off his jacket to drape it around a young pregnant woman who was shaking with the aftereffects of the trauma. Next to the woman, an old man in a black felt beret was staring in surprise at his blood-soaked hand. Mechanically, Phillipa picked up a paper napkin from the glass-littered pavement and began to dab at his gnarled fingers.

Just as the ringing in her ears was diminishing, screaming sirens took its place. The scene was chaotic, with onlookers hindering, more than helping, the wounded. A lone, white-uniformed traffic patrolman was trying to keep the growing crowd under control, ordering them to move back. Feeling terribly disoriented, Phillipa almost sagged with relief when two ambulances arrived and attendants poured out to take charge of the situation.

A man, identifying himself as a newspaperman, was edging through the crowd, and Giles took her by the hand, pulling her in the opposite direction. "Let's get out of here. We don't need my mug on the front of a national daily like the *Constantine World Post.*"

Somehow she managed to find her parked BMW and wedge it through the crush of bystanders. She was surprised to find her hands trembling on the steering wheel. At a stoplight she looked down and saw that dark scarlet speckled her rose-colored skirt.

Giles withdrew a silk handkerchief from the breast pocket of his navy blue blazer and leaned over to dab at her cheek. "You're bleeding."

Her breath caught, with him so near, his eyes grazing her face. "I don't remember being hit," she murmured.

His half smile was remorseful. "I hit you. Or rather, you hit the pavement." His handkerchief lingered at her cheek. "Your skin is more scratched than cut."

Behind her, the frustrated beep of a truck horn warned her that the light had changed. Even at that time of the afternoon the traffic was horrible. "Do you think the MPA was responsible for the bomb?" she asked as she maneuvered the reliable little BMW in and out of the crawling line of cars.

"Definitely, and it wasn't a random attack."

"What do you mean?" She glanced over to find him watching her closely.

"I think there's a possibility the MPA may have mistaken me for Damon when I left the National Palace. After all, I was in his limo, and he and I are the same height and coloring."

She sucked in her breath with surprise. "I hadn't thought of that."

"Of course," he continued calmly, "there could be another explanation."

As they reached the suburbs the traffic was thinning out, and she felt safe to spare a glance at Giles. His light blue trousers were unwrinkled, and his tawny hair was neatly in place, as if he had just blown it dry. No one would have suspected he had just survived a terrorist attack. "Which is?"

"That the attack was meant for me to begin with. Who else knew I was to meet you here?"

"No one."

"No one? You're certain of that?"

"Of course. You and I only made our plans this—" She broke off, bit her lip, then admitted, "Father Murphy did call just before I left the house this morning, and I told him I was meeting you after I left Sophie."

When Giles made no remark she said, "Father Murphy couldn't have done it. Personalities aside, he has no motive."

"If an agent could identify the opposition on motives alone, his job would be much easier."

Turning off onto the private, oak-shaded road leading to Arcadia, she let out a tired little sigh. "If you don't mind, Giles, I think I'll skip dinner this evening. I still feel a little shaky. I think I'll wash the glass out of my hair and go to bed."

"It's been rather a difficult day all around. I still have some plans to go over, for a dam project in the Rhodope Valley, and Major Veranos is arguing for funds to be allocated for a better commando training facility."

She switched off the engine and hesitantly touched his shoulder in a sympathetic gesture. "I forgot that you're trying to do two jobs at once, and I haven't made things any easier for you. I have to admit I was resentful when I learned I would have to work with you. You seemed such a—" she smiled wryly "—male chauvinist."

"Resentful?" he said with a thin smile. "You've been downright defiant. But I freely admit to being a male chauvinist. My father's fault, I'm afraid. He convinced me and my brothers that the man should be the final authority in his household. To be otherwise was considered weak willed."

"Well, I could never accuse you of that."

He glanced down at her hand, then looked back up at her intently. "You are a very lovely woman, Phillipa...in all ways."

She shrank from his scrutiny and averted her face, grateful for the dappled shade of the oaks and the velvet dusk that softened reality. "You're staring."

"I'm staring because I like your face. Very much. You don't look like one of those mannequins in a store window. A plastic model without lines, without a past, without character."

She smiled tightly. "Most women of a certain age have those...qualities."

Rather than try to flatter her, he said, "How old are you, Phillipa?"

"That's rather a rude question from a supposed gentlemen."

"I could always run a check on you through Interpol, you know," he joked, and she knew he was trying to make her relax. "A decrepit old woman like yourself has surely committed enough sins in her lifetime to warrant a record with them."

A small, self-deprecating smile tugged at her lips. "Let's put it this way, Giles. I imagine I have clothes as old as you."

With a charming grin, he said, "Thirty-two years is a long time to rathole a dress."

She chuckled in spite of herself. "Compared to forty-six, thirty-two is nothing."

He clasped her chin in his palm and tilted it, as if to better study her face. "Haven't you heard that a beautiful woman—like you—is ageless?"

"I don't feel beautiful," she said bluntly, honestly. Then she sighed and, lowering her lashes against his scrutiny, admitted, "I feel old, Giles. Half of me feels dead already."

He released her chin and shook his finger at her in a chiding manner. "Phillipa, I know post debutantes who look far—"

She shook her head, unable to articulate her loneliness. "Please, the last thing an older woman needs is a sympathetic shoulder from a younger man."

She moved to slide out of the car, and he grasped her wrist, holding her immobile. "Stop being so defensive, Phillipa, and listen to what I have to say."

She faced him fully. The BMW seemed awfully confining. Her knees were almost touching his. "All right. What do you want to tell me?"

He waited a long time, it seemed to her, looking at her face. In *his* face she saw what in any other man's might be labeled as a momentary lack of self-assurance, but surely not in this arrogant young stallion's.

As if he had made up his mind about something, he finally said in that marvelously rich Welsh voice, "You remind me of a flower, Phillipa—lying concealed in the soil, waiting for the rain to fall on it so that it can burst out and enrich the landscape with its dazzling perfection. I want to be your rain...I want very badly to make love to you."

"Damn," she muttered, angry at herself for being weakened by his words. She loosened her wrist from his grasp and opened the car door, but looked back over her shoulder. "Tell me," she said steadily, "is 'desperate for a man' written somewhere on my forehead?"

"No, but your eyes betray your loneliness. And I'm lonely, too," he said gravely. "The coming together of two such people—to keep loneliness at bay, if even momentarily—isn't such a sin, is it?"

Rage simmered in her blood. "I may be lonely," she said, spacing her words for reinforcement, "but I'm not asking for solace in bed. Go find some young thing to play the stud for. When you mature, Giles Hayes-David, you'll learn what men like Damon know—that easing the loneliness of the soul requires far more than just a romp in bed!"

His lips compressed in a razor-thin line. "I apologize for what appears to have been an insult. I won't raise the subject again."

She watched him stride across the graveled drive and climb the villa's wide steps. She had destroyed his dignity, but preserved her own.

Had it been worth it?

Yes, she thought sadly, walking with lagging footsteps in his wake. Giles would find other conquests to restore his male ego. But if she had succumbed to his blandishments, after the affair had run its course she would never have recovered her fragile sense of self-worth—or the wholeness of her heart.

Chapter 7

White-kilted, red-capped *Evzones* of the Royal Guard were posted at either side of the gate of the centuries-old palazzo in the Thessalonian foothills. Phillipa gave her name to one of the machine-gun-armed guards, and he waved her BMW on past the guard station. A camera mounted in the wall recorded her entrance.

The process seemed slightly insufficient for protecting the family of Macedonia's leader, but Sigourney had assured Phillipa that there was more to the villa's security than met the eye. Sigourney preferred the seclusion the palazzo offered her and her family to the bustle of the capital. "I want my children to grow up in as normal an environment as possible—without constant exposure to the prying eyes of the international media."

Sigourney herself greeted Phillipa at the palazzo's massively ornate double doors, kissing her on the cheek and hugging her affectionately. The Eurasian beauty was wearing a knee-length tunic of blossom-printed red silk that set off her exotic features.

As usual, Phillipa felt a little too tailored, almost stuffy, in her white crepe de chine blouse and suit of Spanish ocher.

"Father Murphy stopped by," Sigourney told her. "He's in the garden with the children. Come on back to the terrace. We can all have high tea there."

Phillipa hadn't known that Father Murphy would be joining them for tea, and she had wanted to talk with Sigourney about intimate...well, women talk, for one thing.

She followed the sleek, dark-haired woman down a cool, arched corridor adorned with Renaissance tapestries, statuary and portraits, along with a head-high ceremonial Indian elephant made of gilded wood. Most of the collections in the palazzo were gifts from foreign governments and other heads of state.

On the terrace, the sudden late afternoon sunlight was momentarily blinding after the palazzo's dim interior. Shielding her eyes with her forearm, Phillipa glanced around. The grounds were in lovely disorder, with the fragrant scents of lemon balm, rosemary and lavender filling the warm afternoon air. A blue stone path meandered down to a cherub-adorned fountain, where two toddlers played. Their sunny laughter filled the garden.

Nearby, on a low, mossy marble bench, Father Murphy hovered like a guardian angel, except angels were supposed to be beautiful, and never had there been a more unlikely candidate for dazzling male beauty than the dear old priest. In a way it would almost be easier to share her troubles with him, for at least he was a part of the dangerous charade in which she and Giles were involved.

At the sight of her he waved a chubby hand and, gathering his black cassock, rose and lumbered up the path to the flagstone terrace. It was an imposing setting, with graceful loggias flanked by Ionic columns and classical statues of Aphrodite and Hera. In front of a stone escutcheon bearing an ancient coat of arms was a white wrought-iron table set with a centerpiece of freshly cut larkspur in a Waterford vase.

A woman in white stockings and apron pushed a trolley across the terrace, rattling the silver tea service she was bringing. Father Murphy, seated opposite Phillipa, exclaimed, "English tea! Sigourney, my child, you've outdone yourself, as usual."

She smiled, her love of the old man obvious in her face. "I thought you two would enjoy the change. All we're missing is crumpets, right, Phillipa?"

"Crumpets are one thing I can afford to miss, Sigourney. When forty came and went, so did my resistance to weight gain."

Father Murphy pumped his thick, grizzled brows up and down. "You lose another pound, my daughter, and you'll look like you did when you came out of Toridallos."

Involuntarily she shuddered. "I'd prefer a jet set spa, thank you."

A cloud momentarily shadowed the garden, as if, Phillipa thought, in concurrence with the somber mood that had settled over the table at the mention of Toridallos.

Sigourney glanced at her two sons and muttered, "I hope Toridallos is something today's Macedonian children never have to experience."

"Ahh, hope," Father Murphy put in. "'Hope is that feeling you have that isn't permanent.'" His jowls quivered with humor. "Jean Kerr supposedly said that."

Phillipa knew he had meant to lighten the mood, but, as Giles had instructed earlier that morning, she brought up the subject of the terrorist bombing, anyway. "You heard about the bombing of the sidewalk café yesterday—the one opposite the National Park?" she asked Sigourney.

"Damon told me about it last night, and then I read about it in this morning's paper." Sigourney's perfect brows met over the bridge of her nose. "He had expected such attacks to increase in frequency the closer it got to the Midsummer Midnight festivities. I'm just relieved no one was killed."

Phillipa watched her friend closely as she said, "Giles and I just happened to be there when it occurred."

The tea in Sigourney's cup sloshed over the gold rim. "Damon didn't tell me that!"

She seemed sincerely astonished, and Phillipa was relieved that Giles's suspicions were obviously groundless.

"Leave it to a man to forget something that important!" Sigourney continued. Her eyes narrowed in mock disgust, and she asked rhetorically, "Is there anything men *are* good for, Father Murphy?"

The misshapen old priest glanced at the two children romping in the garden and mused, "You must admit, men are half responsible for the beautiful children women have."

"Ahh, but if men could get pregnant, Father Murphy," Phillipa teased, "I assure you, divorce would become a sacrament."

The priest's belly rolled with laughter. When his mirth had subsided, he set his cup in his saucer. "I believe I had best leave, my children, before I let the male sex down any further!"

While Sigourney walked Father Murphy to the front door, Phillipa watched Stephanos, who was three, and Christos, a four-year-old version of his father. The toddlers' fleeting interest was momentarily focused on a toad that had hopped from the concealment of the tangled ivy wreathing the base of the fountain. Squealing with delight, they wobbled after it.

Behind her, from the terrace doorway, Sigourney said, "Those two are impossible." She chuckled, a low sound of contentment that Phillipa didn't exactly envy, but certainly longed to know for herself.

"Stephanos has your dark beauty, you know," Phillipa said.

Sigourney slipped back into her chair with that easy grace peculiar to her. "This morning Stephanos took all the goldfish out of the fountain and laid them on the tiled rim, because he thought they must get tired of swimming! Fortunately for them, most of them flopped back into the water."

"That proves that Stephanos was really thinking— he's intelligent, Sigourney." Phillipa adored the two boys. They were the children she would never have.

"You miss not having had children, don't you, Phillipa?" Sigourney asked softly.

Without taking her gaze off the two boys, Phillipa nodded.

"More tea?" Sigourney asked.

"No...thank you."

"You know, Phillipa, your life isn't over. I really believe that somewhere in the world there's another man, the only man meant just for you."

"And what if I don't meet him?"

"You will."

She fixed Sigourney with a long stare of misery. "What assurance do I have that he'll feel the same?"

"How could he not? For one thing, you're strikingly, stunningly lovely."

She smiled wanly. "That sounds like a weapon. Striking, stunning."

Sigourney ignored her. "You're intelligent, pleasant to be around, moderately wealthy—my God, you're even titled!"

"So where is this man?"

For once the famed journalist, the mistress of a thousand words, seemed at a loss. "Well..." she said, attempting a rather weak smile, "maybe your expectations are too high, Phillipa. You know, if you wait until everything's perfect before you remarry, you could be well into senility."

At that Phillipa had to laugh. Sigourney's youth could be contagious. Turning serious again, Phillipa said, "I'd settle for someone my age."

"Surely you've met men your age who seemed special."

"Don't you understand, Sigourney?" she said, a little bit more grimly than she intended. "At my age, men my age seldom come with the territory.'"

Taut with nerves, Phillipa sat in her car in front of a row of the modern duplexes occupied by the employees of the military installation. A car, a dark blue Renault, was slowing down on the fluorescent-lit street, as if prepared to stop.

It did worse. It turned into a driveway two duplexes away from where Phillipa was parked—Melina's! The girl was supposed to have been in an afterwork meeting called by Damon, but it had obviously ended much sooner than Giles had counted on.

Phillipa sounded her horn, three short beeps, to alert Giles, who was inside Melina's house, installing a tap on the telephone. Melina parked her car and got out, leaning forward against the wind that whipped her taxicab-yellow plastic raincoat. All too soon she would find that her front door was no longer locked.

Dear Lord, what if she glimpsed the flashlight beams through the window?

Unconsciously Phillipa held her breath as Melina pushed the door open. Immediately a wedge of light spilled out over her where she still stood on the porch, telling Phillipa that Melina must be suspicious if she had remained outside to turn on the inside light. She was no doubt surveying the room before going inside.

Apparently satisfied, the woman entered, and Phillipa waited tensely for whatever might happen next. How would Giles explain his presence?

The same way he explained his presence in your bathroom. By seducing you with a kiss.

Phillipa wiped her sweaty palms together, unable to bear the waiting. If only she could walk, pace the street, anything other than just sitting.

Unexpectedly Melina reappeared on her porch. She walked quickly to the car and got in, then started up the engine. No sooner had she pulled out of the driveway than Giles, dressed in black trousers and a black Windbreaker over a dark T-shirt, came loping out of the house.

"What happened?" Phillipa asked when he slid into the seat beside her. As always, his presence filled her car. His maleness was a veiled threat to her resolve to remain aloof.

He returned the flashlight to her glove compartment. "She got a phone call just after she walked inside. Let's go. Follow her, and I'll tell you the rest."

Silently cursing, Phillipa pulled out behind Melina. She knew nothing about tailing another car. "How far behind her do I stay?"

"About a hundred meters. I was in the back bedroom, monitoring the telephone call. A male voice said to meet him at the The Golden Drachma in an hour, room 214. Whoever it was didn't even bother to introduce himself."

"Not an ordinary call, then."

"Hardly. When we get out on the highway—"

"How do you know she'll be using the highway?"

"If it were someplace close, in Melpomene, she wouldn't have been in a hurry, not with an hour to spare. Once we're on the highway, leave a greater distance between our car and hers, and alternate lanes. That should help throw off any possible suspicions that she might be being tailed."

"I'm impressed with your knowledge of surveillance," Phillipa snapped, finally allowing her relief that he was safe to flood through her.

"I credit the British Secret Service for whatever knowledge I may have acquired," he said, mild humor in his voice.

"For all the good it might do you," she threw back at him. "You could have gotten yourself shot as a burglar back there. You were just lucky."

He rubbed his knuckle along her neck in a seductive gesture. "Were you concerned for me?"

"You know damned well I was." Then, in defense, she qualified her statement. "If you had been caught, our operation could have been blown."

"Your concern is gratifying," he said dryly.

"Look. Isn't that Melina's car? The one pulling off the road?"

"Keep going. She's either suspicious or just taking the precaution of checking for a tail. About a mile up ahead, wherever there are some trees, ease off the highway. We'll wait for her to pass us."

Phillipa slowed down a short distance later, turned off the highway and rolled to a stop near a clump of what appeared, in the dark, to be twisted olive trees. The wind, like a spiteful spirit, tossed their branches eerily. "I just can't believe that Melina would betray us."

"Anything is possible," he muttered.

Within a minute, at the most, what looked like Melina's dark blue Renault passed them at high speed, along with a cluster of several other cars. Phillipa let them get several hundred meters ahead, then pulled back onto the highway. The pavement was iridescent with a mist that both bespoke a slippery surface and promised a drenching downpour.

"Which car belongs to Melina?" she asked, hating to admit that she had lost sight of the Renault on the mist-darkened highway.

"It's the third one ahead in the right lane."

"How can you tell?" she asked peevishly. "At this distance the cars all look alike."

She detected the subtle amusement in his voice. "I took the precaution of marking Melina's car when I was last there. I sprayed a small area on the rear fender with a can of liquid glass. It works wonders."

"I see the reflection now." She tried not to think about what had gone on that night. Melina was young, fresh, exactly the kind of woman a man Giles's age needed. Giles deserved a wife and his own children, something Phillipa knew she could never give him.

"Giles, look! Melina is taking the exit to Tipraeus."

The Renault made straight for the wharf, the roughest part of any seaport. Phillipa and Giles watched Melina park on the esplanade above the wharf, then become quickly lost in the crowd. "You stay here," Giles said.

Phillipa grabbed his sleeve as he moved to get out of the car. "You're not going without me, Giles. We're a team, remember?"

His face stern, he removed her hand from his sleeve. "You're not going. It isn't safe."

"Either I go with you, or I go without you, but I *am* going."

In the dark of the car his eyes shot blue flames. "You're a hardheaded woman. My father would have taken you over his knee for your insubordination."

"I'm not in the military, Giles. I am an independent consultant for Macedonia and Damon, and I don't have to obey orders."

At the mention of Damon, he muttered some imprecation she didn't quite catch. "Let's go," he said grudgingly. He took her hand again and helped her out of the car. "We're wasting time."

How could just the touch of his hand, larger and stronger than hers, thrill her so? Her heels tapped rapidly down the oil-stained concrete ramp as he pulled her after him. Lightning forked above dimly lit shanties and seedy taverns that conspired with the fog coming in off the Aegean to conceal whatever nefarious deeds were being perpetrated along the wharfside. Only the lowest echelons of society consorted here. Sailors from all nations jostled with the dockside prostitutes for room to walk—or stagger, for the more inebriated.

Ahead of them, she thought she caught sight of Melina, wending her way through the press of seamen and their doxies. Then Phillipa lost sight of her, if she had seen Melina at all.

A moment later Giles swerved into a doorway, above which hung a sign, The Golden Drachma. The place appeared to be a combination hotel and dive. Inside the room was dense with smoke and smelled of cheap cigars, bile, stale beer and human sweat. The place was packed with customers standing and sitting at lilliputian tables.

"Stay with me," he grunted beneath his breath.

She darted a glance at the raucous sailors, who looked as if they were spoiling for a fight, and the muscle-heavy longshoremen, who looked willing to accommodate them. She moved a little closer to Giles's tall, prepossessing frame. "A crowbar couldn't pry me away."

"Do you see Melina?" The shouting and laughter were so loud that Phillipa could barely hear him.

"No." But then it was awfully difficult trying to peer through the cloud of smoke. Still, with her fluorescent yellow raincoat, the woman should have been easy to spot.

"There's the stairwell," Giles said. "Behind that row of booths."

She followed Giles closely, letting him shoulder a path through the sardine-packed sailors toward a stairway that had only a portion of its wooden railing remaining. Other customers were also going upstairs, usually with a female companion in tow.

When Giles reached the landing, its dirty bulb shedding only muted light, he halted before the door marked 214, and she almost collided with him. "This time, Phillipa, you stay outside."

He tried the doorknob. The door opened easily, and he stepped inside, leaving her alone in the hallway. Only then did she notice that it smelled of human sweat and other unnameable odors. She could think of a thousand places she would rather be. Without waiting another moment, she stepped inside the room, immediately behind Giles.

"What the—"

Both she and Giles stared mutely at the couple thrashing on the bed in the throes of lovemaking: Melina and Gregorios Zychapoulos.

Giles nudged Phillipa back outside. Leaning against the hall wall, their mouths compressed to hold their laughter in, they finally dared to meet each other's eyes. Unable to maintain a sober expression any longer, she had to smother her laughter with the back of her hand. Then Giles began to laugh, and she was lost.

"So much for our expertise at tracking down traitors," she gasped between barely stifled giggles.

On the drive back to Constantine she felt more lighthearted than she had in days. The restraint between her and Giles was gone, replaced by a tenuous camaraderie. Moreover, Melina had been ruled out as the prime suspect—and as Giles's love interest.

That the latter eased Phillipa's mind more than the former caused her no little self-recrimination. After all, why should she care whether Giles was involved with someone, much less who that someone was?

Chapter 8

"The gentle girl with the golden hair,
Golden is the burden that you carry on your head.
White is your body, and slim,
And you shine with it. What a gift!"

Finished with reciting the poem, Giles grinned somewhat shyly and leaned forward to pat the well-muscled neck of the chestnut Thoroughbred he rode. His Welsh eloquence and that rare shy grin made Phillipa's heart beat erratically.

"And that, my dear, is a translation of our medieval Welsh poet, Dafydd ap Gwilym. He was a lyric genius in Chaucer's time, but, of course, the translation loses much of the effect."

"I gather he was also something of a ladies' man," she teased.

"All Welshmen are, from Dylan Thomas to Richard Burton."

"Including yourself, of course?"

He cast her a glance full of mock lechery. "Can't you tell? Actually, I imagine I'm more of a bard than a ladies' man."

They dismounted to walk their horses along one of the secluded trails crisscrossing Arcadia's sprawling, bucolic grounds, which were nearly as vast as Constantine's Old Town. It was the 20th of July, Midsummer Midnight, and the entire country was shut down for the national holiday, forcing Giles to slow his own adrenaline-charged pace. She was grateful for the respite from the razor-edged tension of their concentrated espionage.

It had been his suggestion to exercise her neglected horses. His balance in the saddle indicated that he wasn't the best of riders, but he handled his mount with the assurance and confidence typical of all that he undertook.

The afternoon was sultry, with the threat of late afternoon thunderstorms, and the humid air was sweet with the raw scent of summer. She removed the scarf she wore around her neck, dabbing at the perspiration pooling in the hollow of her throat.

Giles was dressed rather eclectically in Australian Outback fatigues, cowboy boots and a carnelian polo shirt. Its rolled-up sleeves and open throat exposed rich

brown hair matting skin darkly tanned by the fierce
Baghrashi sun. But then she imagined that Giles had
probably seen duty in other desert and tropical countries, too.

She knew far too little about the Welshman. Oh,
there was the obvious: his male beauty and physique
were phenomenal, and his eyes, the cool blue of a
fjord, glittered with an uncanny perception that she
found unnerving.

Over the weeks she had discovered other small, revealing things about him. His cynicism barely masked
a deep sentimentality. His clipped Welsh voice, like his
glacial reserve, grew softer and more human as the day
wore on. At times his Celtic passion thundered and
brooded. And, like herself, he possessed a deep rever-
ence for British tradition and was as proud of his own
distinguished lineage as she was of hers.

She did know that he seemed almost inhuman, too
perfect, too capable. She needed a weakness, a vice, a
fear—something that would make him less interesting
to her, less attractive. Living with him under such intimate circumstances only intensified the profound effect he had on her, rather than mitigating it.

In this case familiarity had not bred contempt. She
was terribly afraid that one of Father Murphy's favorite quotes, "Familiarity breeds consent," would prove
all too true in her situation. The only way she was going
to keep from making a fool of herself over Giles was to
somehow diffuse the sexual tension building between
them and maintain the tenuous camaraderie the two of

them shared, at least until the undercover operation was over and he went merrily on his way.

Lately, whenever he approached, she would go suddenly still. Nervous perspiration would begin to bead on her upper lip. In her ears she would hear her accelerated heartbeat thudding warningly, and her mouth would become as dry as the desert Giles had known, so that she felt the betraying need to clear her throat before attempting speech.

She cleared her throat now. "Do you ever think about working at a normal job, Giles, instead of this...this troubleshooting all over the world?"

Against his golden tan his teeth were brilliant. "Believe it or not, I always had a secret yearning to write novels. But royalties rarely pay the bills, not unless the author is lucky enough to produce a blockbuster. I'm afraid it would take several blockbusters to keep Cambria in operation."

"Cambria is that important to you?"

"Rather. I suppose I am tied to the land, the soil, even its history. But it's more than that. Like your Rothingham, Cambria—meaning myself—is responsible for almost two hundred families who depend on it one way or another for their livelihoods. Gone are the dead slag heaps, and in their place are two small modern factories."

She was impressed, and her voice showed it. "How did you manage to achieve all that?"

"It wasn't easy. When I realized I might never escape the coal mines I did what Dylan Thomas only dreamed of—sailed from Swansea, a harbor of high romance, on a rusty tramp steamer. I saved enough money to finish a prep school education. The scholarship I told you about provided entrée into Oxford. There I met Khalid Rajhi. Later, after I left the Secret Service, his uncle, the emir of Baghrashi, made me an offer I couldn't refuse."

"Which was?"

"An enormous amount of money that would both pay for Cambria's costly maintenance and its even costlier refurbishing, along with financing certain industrial projects I had in mind for the town." He grinned ruefully. "After only two weeks in that backward but barrenly beautiful Arab country, I began to realize why old Sheikh Ibrahim Rajhi was so munificent. He had nothing to give but sand."

"Tell me, Giles, why have you waited so long to marry?" She hadn't meant to sound so abrupt. The question had just slipped unbidden off her traitorous tongue.

He shoved back a sweat-dampened lock of hair that had tumbled across his forehead. "Well, I suppose I'm not into self-sacrifice."

"I find that rather difficult to believe. Look what you've done for the tenants of Cambria. Introducing industry and bringing in tourism."

"Don't attribute lofty ideals to me, Phillipa. You could also call what I did self-serving. Only by doing all that was I able to preserve my heritage and Cambria."

He swung around to face her, so that his horse blocked the bridle path. In the leafy shadows his eyes were as dark and sultry as the steamy air. "I'm not your selfless Damon, Phillipa."

She looked away into the surrounding forest. A timid squirrel scampered down a tree trunk to take a curious peek at the intruders, then scampered away. "Is that a warning?"

"In the world of espionage," he said softly, "an agent called a raven is sometimes used to seduce the quarry into his trap."

Her gaze slashed back to his. "Am I your quarry?" she gasped. "Surely you don't suspect *me* of being the Oracle of Delphi?"

He tugged his reins, and their horses moved forward in unison. For a moment the only sound was the crunch of the past winter's dead leaves under their feet. "I did rather seriously entertain the possibility."

The preposterousness of his statement fairly took her breath away. "What changed your mind?" she asked testily. "My delightful derriere, as you put it?"

His mouth curved downward in a wry grimace. "Your delectable anatomy had the ability to sway my opinion considerably, but it was the bombing of the restaurant the other afternoon that really convinced me. If you were the Oracle, you wouldn't have risked being there."

"Believe me," she said passionately, "I want nothing more than to uncover the traitor's identity, not only for Macedonia's sake, for Damon's, but for my own!"

Then, without meaning to, she blurted, "Living with you, pretending we're the adoring brother and sister, is very difficult for me."

"Why?" He was watching her closely.

"Why? Why because it's more like being husband and . . .
Please understand," she implored. "I can't help myself. I hear you shaving in your bathroom in the morning, and, without stopping to think, I imagine for a split second that you're Aaron. Several mornings, when I've been distracted by something or other, I've almost wandered in on you."

He stopped walking altogether. "Then you're not in love with Damon?"

Her eyes flashed with annoyance as she told him what she now knew to be true. "I told you before I wasn't! Dear God," she snapped, "I just want to get this awful farce over with. Then I can leave Macedonia and go home to Rothingham."

She immediately regretted her outburst. She had opened a breach in her wall of defense. In the distance thunder rumbled ominously, and she murmured, "We'd better be getting back to the stable. The summer thundershowers here are more like deluges."

He caught her reins, preventing her from mounting. "Are you certain you know what you want?"

She stared hard at him. "I know what I don't want!"

Then she yanked the reins from his grip and mounted without his assistance. He had no choice but to mount his own horse and follow her. She held to a brisk trot until she reached the stables.

Inside, the sunlight didn't reach the stalls. The warm, heady smell of horse manure and sawdust mixed with hay filled her nostrils. In her mind's eye the deserted stable became the romantic setting for one of the myriad scenes she had seen played out on film.

She dismounted too quickly, bent on fleeing the stables as hastily as was possible. The toe of her riding boot caught in the stirrup, and she went sprawling in the dust ignominiously. At once Giles was at her side, kneeling on one knee. "Are you all right?"

She nodded her head in the affirmative, feeling miserable. "Only my pride hurts," she said with a halfhearted attempt at an apologetic smile.

He took her gloved hands and pulled her to her feet, but he didn't release her. Instead, he drew her hands to his chest, so that she was forced to stand close to him. He bent to kiss her lips, very, very lightly, and her lids drifted closed. Helplessly she trembled, as if in the throes of fever.

The kiss was over in a second. He lifted his head and said, "I wouldn't hurt you, Phillipa."

Dumbstruck, she stared up into his solemn face. She was helpless, quivering and bewildered, feeling like someone whose life had been changed forever in the space of a second. With a gradually dawning horror she realized that she was intensely and supremely in love with this Welshman. The love she felt for him was totally different from the love she had felt for Aaron, and from the quiet passion she had carried within her for Damon all these years.

Her love for Giles was a wild fury, a high-voltage burst, an assault on all her senses, of the sort that she had thought would never happen to the oh-so-proper Lady Phillipa Fleming.

She wiped the back of her hand across her forehead, as if by that action she could completely wipe Giles Hayes-David from her mind. She struggled for sanity. "Affairs are temporary, and that would make me feel so...so degraded."

He released his hold on her and thrust his hands in the pockets of his jeans. The clipped Welsh accent was back in his voice. "Well, milady, you can look for your nice, neat idea of life in the ladies' magazines, but real life is not that way. Life is messy, without guarantees. However, while you're looking we can act like friends...like virgins."

"Your humor is...ill placed." She backed away a step, then turned and hurried from the building.

Obviously, sleep was not going to come easily. She tossed the sheet off and rolled onto her stomach. Her slit-legged negligee had ridden up around her thighs, sticking to her clammy skin. And her eyes felt sandpapery from lack of sleep.

She opened her eyes, not wanting to glimpse the erotic scene stamped on the back of her lids: Giles, asleep on his bed, his beautiful body exposed to her gaze.

Giles.

She knew it was a mistake to let him slip into her thoughts at night, such a dangerously weak time for her. She turned over onto her back, arms crossed behind her head, and stared into the darkness. Lightning flashed through the room; then the thunderstorm that had been threatening burst and pelted her bedroom windows with raindrops.

Raising herself on one elbow, she turned on the small bedside lamp and picked up a bestselling mystery from her nightstand. Several times she had tried to start it, but she just hadn't been able to get into it.

She thought about Giles and his desire to write. She thought she had an instinct about such things, and she believed he would be an excellent writer. He was articulate and resourceful and, obviously, well-read.

The words on the page were beginning to run together when a loud clap of thunder erupted, startling her fully awake. Lightning followed on the thunder's heels. The entire room was illuminated as if it were daylight. Then the lamp went out, leaving her in total darkness.

With a sigh she swung her feet over the edge of the bed and padded across the carpet to her dresser, where she kept a flashlight in a drawer with her scarves for just such emergencies.

At the pounding on her door, which these days she remembered to keep closed, she whirled and stared with wide-eyed distress across the intervening space.

"Phillipa?" Giles shouted.

She broke out of her catatonic daze and flung open the door to confront him. A flash of lightning illuminated his powerful golden body, naked and glistening with sweat. He seemed oblivious to his nudity. "A flashlight?" he snapped, his sweat-sheened chest rising and falling with his shallow breathing. "Do you have a flashlight anywhere? Or a candle? Matches? Anything?"

"Yes," she said uncertainly.

With an effort she dragged her nervous gaze away from the potent attraction he presented.

She crossed to the dresser to rummage through her drawer for the flashlight. Without actually hearing him, she knew that he had come up behind her. She had only to sway slightly to touch him.

"Here it is," she murmured, and turned abruptly to collide with him. The flashlight clattered on the floor. "Dammit," she muttered and knelt to grope for it.

He crouched beside her, his sweat-dampened hand closing over hers. "Phillipa."

She froze. Any response died in her throat. How could her skin be so cold and her blood so hot?

He pulled her up against him, so that they were knee to knee on the floor, her silk-clad breasts pressed against the muscled wall of his chest. His hand tunneled through her short curls, and he growled, "Hold me. Just hold me."

Astonished, she did as he'd bade, wrapping her arms over his wide shoulders. His flesh was feverish beneath her hands; his skin goosepimpled; the hairs on his arms erect. When she felt his muscular neck beneath her probing fingers, she trembled with a sensation she had long forgotten.

"What is it, my love?" she whispered against his throat, only half aware of the words of endearment she had used.

He swallowed. "The lights—I need you, Phillipa." His voice was anguished, and he buried his face in the hollow of her neck. His breath was hot against her skin.

That Giles, who seemed to fear no man, should have such a terrible fear of the dark astounded Phillipa. Later she would get him to explain his fear, tell her of whatever childhood horrors he must have experienced to create such an abnormal response to the dark. "I'm here, my love," she said simply. "I'm here."

As if reassuring himself that she was indeed there, he began to run his lips over her shoulder, her face, frantically and softly. Then, as though he had come to his senses, his lips slowed their conquest and gently, leisurely, moved down the curve of her breast above the lace of her nightgown.

All hope of preserving her dignity was lost. In his arms, beneath his kisses, she was discovering that secret of human passion that she had never known. "Please..." she groaned. "Oh, Giles...please take me. Get this wanting over with."

He said nothing, but pulled her to the floor with the haste of a lover too long denied. With clumsy, fumbling movements he literally tore her nightgown from her, and she didn't care. She wanted him so badly. When his golden head lowered, his mouth raining kisses on the gentle curve of her belly, her fingers gripped his shoulders, and he understood her immediate need.

He moved over her and thrust deep inside her, so that she felt as if he filled her completely. Then her body began to match the tempo of his, a perfect union between two souls. Her hands pressed marvelingly against his back, followed the strong line of his spine, cupped his firm buttocks.

Intermittent flashes of lightning flickered over their sweat-sheened, interlocked bodies. Above her, his face was feral with his need for her. She felt him throbbing with passion, exploding too soon, leaving her still craving the thrust and pull of him.

"Oh, Phillipa, keep still," he muttered. "Just wait a minute."

He remained inside her, his face inches from hers, gently kissing her cheeks with moist, sensuous lips. Then he began to run his lips between her breasts, lifting his tawny head to circle her nipples with a tongue that was soft. She groaned, and her fingers tunneled through his hair, holding him close, as he laved her breasts.

Her eyes fluttered closed. "Oh, Giles," she murmured almost incoherently. "I never knew I could feel like this! That...a man's body...mine...could feel this good."

"It's only just beginning," he promised her in a voice that was husky with a passion yet to be slaked.

When he moved within her once again, she felt flooded with the urgency of her passion. Then he made love to her, really made love to her, a slow purposeful entering and withdrawing, a stroking of her spirit as well as her body.

As he loved her, he raised himself on his elbows and clutched her hands while his eyes gazed into hers, leaving her helpless with pulsating desire. Her breasts felt full and heavy, her nipples erect, thrusting forward aggressively. For the first time in her life she felt totally feminine, devoid of shame, abandoned to love.

She could only murmur, "Yes...yes...yes!" She pleaded incoherently with him to continue the wild things his lips and tongue and fingers were doing.

Suddenly her body was racked by paroxysms of painfully intense pleasure. She was discovering her own rhythm, a rhythm that had waited, hidden in her body, until this moment in time. After the little convulsions subsided she astonished herself, and Giles, by beginning to cry. She was unable to stop sobbing. Tears of joy cascaded from her tightly closed eyes.

"Hush, love," Giles murmured in bewilderment. Still lying half over her, he stroked her sweat-dampened curls. "It's all right."

She doubted if he or any man could totally understand what she was feeling, so all she said was, "I know. It *is* all right." She hiccupped and gingerly wiped the tears from her face with the back of her hand. Her cheeks and lips were tender, rasped by his beard-shadowed face.

In his smile she caught that knowing expression all men have when they feel they have truly pleasured a woman, but that look was tempered by the way his eyes moved over her face with a marveling gaze. "I feel aeons older than you, Phillipa." His finger traced the curve of her lips as if they were wondrously formed. "You seem so very, very young to me."

She should have been pleased, but the thought came to her, What if their paths had never crossed? How had she endured so long without this? Without him?

Chapter 9

Philippa's jaw tightened, and unshed tears glistened in her eyes. "I wasn't a very good wife, Father Murphy."

She had realized that fact only now. All those years when she had been married, she had withheld a very vital part of herself from Aaron.

"By whose definition?" he grumbled. "Some silly manual on how to please your man?"

She and the old priest were sitting in her car, parked across the street from the National Palace, while they waited for a luncheon rendezvous with Giles. At the mere thought of him memories of the night before besieged her.

In the light of day she was astonished by her lack of restraint. Yet, try as she would, she could not forget that he was fourteen years younger than she.

Still, in his hot, sweet kisses, beneath his worshiping hands, she had remembered that there had been joy in being alive. The lips that had stopped her breath had also snatched back into life that part of her that had withdrawn into some cave of lonely existence.

The decisive lines of his face, his serious eyes, his rich Welsh voice had not diminished in her memory since last night. Instead, as she'd awakened that morning, thoughts of Giles Hayes-David had crowded everything else from her mind with an insistence she could not ignore.

And that was the problem. She felt so hypocritical, because it wasn't her possible failure as a wife in the past that assailed her today, but her failure as a woman now. Last night, in the dark, her body had been young and lithe. This morning she was just a confused, struggling middle-age woman with little to show for her years of experience.

I am a woman with a woman's needs! she wanted to shout.

"You're a dear old man," she told the priest, groping for a lace handkerchief in her shoulder bag.

"Old? Oh, no. I don't think of myself as old. I plan to keep my youth as long as possible, ignore middle age altogether and go straight from here to senility."

At that she had to chuckle. "I'm the one who feels old. Look at me! Crying."

He took her handkerchief and dabbed her cheeks. His thick, shaggy brows waggled over sunken eyes that somehow managed to twinkle. "Now, why don't you think you were a good wife, my child?"

She looked away from his discerning gaze and stared, tear blinded, at a white-uniformed policeman, who was directing traffic with the grace of a ballet dancer. She turned her gaze to the cars that were darting through the National Palace's Military Square. Should she risk shocking Father Murphy by telling him the truth about her marriage? But, then, nothing shocked the ugly priest.

Her voice was raspy, low. "Sometimes, Father—most of the time—after Aaron and I . . . made love, I would roll away, grateful that it was over. Much later I'd hear Aaron getting quietly out of bed, wandering around the bedroom, prowling the kitchen. I'd close my eyes, but I would know that he had come back. I could feel him, standing there, staring at me. Sometimes he would touch my hair lightly, so lightly, and, thinking he wanted to make love again, I'd pretend I was asleep. Dear God, I understand now—too late—he was just lonely. He just wanted to communicate. I never really bothered to understand him!" It was an anguished cry.

Father Murphy leaned as close to her as his corpulence would allow and patted her hand. "Are you confessing to being human, my daughter? Such a dreary trait. I had hoped you could entertain me with sins that weren't so repetitive of the ones I've heard over the years."

Her mouth, struggling—like her mind—between sobriety and laughter, gave in to the latter and crimped upward. "You're not taking me seriously, Father!"

"Oh, but I promise you, I'm taking you very seriously, as I do all confessions. As for your problem with your late husband, it's quite common, really. 'The reason husbands and wives don't understand each other is because they belong to different sexes.' Dorothy Dix said that."

"I love you, you old bear. And my handkerchief is positively sopping. Whatever will Giles think?"

"I'd loan you my cassock's hem, but it's a little coarse for wiping noses of damsels in distress. And wretchedly hot in this heat. If hell is worse than this, I shall just have to make a better effort at ministering to my flock."

"Father! That car—the green coupe there, stopped for traffic! Look. Its rear window—it's broken!"

"That one? Yes, I see the window. But what's so incredible about—"

"No, I mean that's the car the bomb was hurled from—the bomb thrown at the sidewalk café last week! Father, you must get out and find Giles. Quickly! Tell him I'm going to follow the coupe. I'll come back for you two as soon as possible."

Although Father Murphy hefted his bulk from the car with extraordinary rapidity, the green automobile had already shot through Military Square. She gunned away from the curb and entered the heavy flow of lunch-hour traffic. Every so often she caught a glimpse of the coupe two or three cars ahead of her.

Having expected the car to turn off the main boulevard and head either for Old Town or one of the ancient capital's ghettos, she was surprised when the coupe continued on the thoroughfare, leaving Constantine itself.

She glanced at her watch. Twenty-five minutes gone. Enough time for her to wonder just who her quarry was. She knew that Giles hadn't altogether ruled out either Melina or Zychapoulos. Both seemed ludicrous suspects to her. She felt that they were two people who had come together merely to assuage the loneliness of their lives.

As had Giles and herself, she thought grimly.

The coupe turned off onto a highway she wasn't familiar with. Where could the car be going? Soon fields, the bright green of summer, replaced the city's modern outskirts and tree-lined side streets. The four-lane boulevard narrowed to two, and the coupe slowed to a more sedate speed to negotiate the curves of the vineyard-terraced hills.

She tried to keep in mind all Giles had told her about tailing a car. She hoped to keep another car, a battered yellow Fiat, between her and the sedan, but eventually the Fiat turned down a dusty side road, scattering chickens as it went. After that she attempted to maintain a steady pace several hundred yards behind her quarry.

At the third or fourth village the coupe came to, a drowsy place of shuttered and whitewashed houses, it turned off the main square. She had to halt to let a straggling line of sheep, shepherded by an old man in a beret and carrying his crook, pass ahead of her. Softly but vehemently, she cursed.

By the time she was able to turn the coupe was nowhere in sight. The road was little wider than her BMW, and cobblestoned. Ahead of her the teeth-jarring street began to climb and dwindle to a wheel-rutted path, with neither automobile nor pedestrian to be seen. She must have lost the coupe back in the village!

She was certain the village was on the Aegean, because even in the closed car she could smell the damp salty air that made her short curls lie limply about her temples. With much shifting of the gears she was able to turn the BMW around and head back into the village.

Now she peered carefully down the streets that intersected with the one she was on. Naturally they were all empty; it was siesta time.

Then she spotted the coupe—parked almost flush with a little box of a house, whose walls were badly cracked and in need of whitewashing. On the flat roof she spied a man, crouching, but the Mediterranean sunlight blinded her, glinting off something he held in his hands, and when she glanced again, he wasn't there.

She certainly wasn't brave enough to get out of her car and do any snooping. She slowed to a halt half a dozen yards behind the coupe and turned off the ignition. She fished in her purse and came up with a small spiral notepad. The license plate was easy enough to read: ZG-153.

When she turned to cram the notepad back into her purse a hand was clamped over her mouth. The car door was yanked open, and another hand latched on to her arm, dragging her from the car.

"Let go of—"

A fleshy palm silenced her outcry.

In her struggle she scraped her calf on the rocker panel and, foolishly, all she could think of was her expensive hosiery, ruined.

She tried to sink her teeth into the sweaty hand covering her mouth. Fingers dug into her jaws brutally. One of her high-heeled sandals fell off, and she saw a short, paunchy man retrieve it. Then she was hauled inside the house. The room's sudden dimness swallowed her.

"Hurry, shut the damned door!" a gravelly voice yelled from behind her.

The breath whooshed from her as she was slammed into a chair. At once a rag, smelling of transmission oil, was stuffed into her mouth and bound by another rag tied behind her head. Her arms were wrenched behind the chair and her wrists tied.

The little flour sack of a man moved to the doorway, and then the shaft of sunlight was obliterated with the closing of the door. "Who is she?"

"You don't recognize her?" the other grunted. "It's her most royal highness, Lady Phillipa."

He knew who she was! The realization injected fear that iced its way up her spinal cord. Her only hope lay in convincing them that she had been innocently observing them. But gagged as she was, that would be a little difficult to achieve.

Gradually, while her ankles were also being roped together, her pupils focused. A naked lightbulb was suspended from the high ceiling, casting a weak, yellowish light on a filthy and faded green-and-white print sofa that was punctured by springs. Plaster peeled from walls that formed a room no larger than her bathroom, maybe fifteen by twenty feet.

Propped in a far corner was a submachine gun with the distinctive curved black magazine and laminated woodwork of an AK-47—if she correctly recollected the information she had been given years before by Damon at the PFF's secret military training camp.

Through an arched doorway she could make out what seemed to be a kitchen of sorts—a portion of a cheap porcelain enamel sideboard, one spindly leg and the corner of a table. Another doorway probably led to a lone bedroom.

Her assailant moved around to join the short man standing before her, arms akimbo, his little mouth pursed. Above her gag her eyes darted like caged swallows from him to the other terrorist, who was bald and of medium height but of brawny build. He had a nose like a ski slope.

All he needed, she thought, was a corncob pipe to look like a malevolent Popeye.

The way the two stared at her... her heart thudded out of control, and sweat flooded her armpits. Too easily she remembered the horrendous forty-eight-hour grilling sessions at Toridallos.

"What do we do with her, Yeorgi?" Flour Sack asked, a nervous sheen of perspiration beading his thick upper lip. He looked middle aged except for his curiously peach-fuzzed cheeks.

"The Oracle won't be happy about this," the man called Yeorgi said in a voice that was half snarl. "Get rid of her car."

"Where?"

"Damn it, I don't care where. Just get rid of it. In the sea."

Obediently Flour Sack waddled to the door. When he opened it, sunlight pierced her eyes, and then the room was once more dim. Alone with Yeorgi, she squirmed uneasily in her bindings. She couldn't bring herself to look into his lashless eyes.

For several minutes he prowled the room, every so often glowering his dislike of her. As if unable to control himself, he turned on her at last. "Tell me, Lady Phillipa, have you been lonely these past few years without your husband in your bed?"

Her gaze slashed upward to his, then ricocheted from the mean look she saw in his headstone-gray irises. She recognized that look, recognized his kind. She had seen it in Toridallos, worn by people small of mind and heart, people who made themselves feel bigger by diminishing the spirit of others.

Slowly Yeorgi circled her, his eyes traveling over her body from her tied ankles upward to linger on her breasts, ludicrously thrust forward by the painful angle of her bound arms. Goose bumps puckered her flesh. The back of his hand, speckled with either freckles or sun spots, brushed back and forth across one breast, and he laughed when she shrank back as far as the chair permitted. The gag muffled her pleading words.

He crouched before her and ran his hand up her calf. "Poor woman. You tore your stocking."

Bile was rising at the back of her throat. Toridallos had been a nightmare of suffering, but at least she hadn't been subjected to sexual assault.

"I'd bet I could make you beg real nice...bet I could make you forget you're a titled lady...make you plead like an Old Town whore."

His fingers clamped about her calf and squeezed. She groaned, and he chuckled softly. He slid his hand over her knee, his fingers crawling beneath the hem of her dress like gross caterpillars, and she went instantly rigid. He had begun to mouth obscenities about what he planned to do to her when the door opened again and the other terrorist entered.

He saw what Yeorgi was up to and asked, "Do you think you should be doing that?" He rubbed his pudgy hands together nervously. "The Oracle might not like it."

"The Oracle doesn't have to know," Yeorgi growled, but he withdrew his hand from her thigh and stood up with a muttered oath.

"Aren't we going to tell him about her?"

"Of course, but he doesn't have to know everything." He fixed the other man with hard eyes. "Like the time you killed the wrong woman."

"But I made up for it, Yeorgi," the other terrorist said in a squeaky, pleading voice. "I tracked down the right one and took—"

"I'm going to make contact with the Oracle now," Yeorgi broke in impatiently. "You watch her—and I mean watch her. Don't even talk to her. Understand?"

Obediently the paunchy terrorist nodded.

After Yeorgi left all the adrenaline that had sustained her subsided, and she went completely limp, her shoulders sagging as far as her bonds—plastic-coated wire of some sort—permitted.

The room was oppressively hot and stuffy and smelled of boiled cabbage and garlic. Sweat rolled off Flour Sack's plump cheeks and down into the folds of his neck. Nervously he paced the dirty floor, roaming into the kitchen and from there into the bedroom, then back.

He avoided looking at her. Once he glanced at the submachine gun, and she wondered in panic what he was thinking. Would the urge to kill her overcome him? He didn't look the type. But then, how many killers did?

He wandered back into the kitchen, and she could hear him moving around in there: the clatter of kitchen utensils; the crinkling of cellophane; the opening and closing of a refrigerator.

With a surge of relief she realized that he was fixing himself something to eat. She had missed lunch, but hunger was the last thing on her mind. She couldn't breathe very well, and with the stench of transmission fluid flooding her nose she felt so dizzy that any attempt at lucid thinking seemed a monumental effort.

She should be planning how she could escape, but the situation appeared hopeless to her. All Father Murphy would be able to tell Giles was that she had tailed a green coupe north on Alexander Boulevard.

In absolute despair she let her head fall forward. She dreaded the return of Yeorgi, if only because of his invading, repugnant hands. She tried to control her imagination, but memories made that virtually impossible.

How ironic. She might soon learn the identity of the Oracle of Delphi, only to die. For surely he wouldn't let her live.

She thought of Giles, setting all her concentration on him. His powerful masculinity had made her feel so utterly feminine; more than that, he was the materialization of a dream she had almost abandoned. She wanted to weep, not for the horror that awaited her, but for the simple joy that was now lost to her and the possibility of his returning her love.

Flour Sack entered the room again, a sandwich made with *kourtura* between his hands. Welcome to reality, she thought. Her shoulders stiffened; her head snapped up; her eyes glared defiantly. His kind preferred the smell of fear—it was easier to deal with—but she refused to give him that pleasure.

Munching loudly on his food, he stared at her with an unhappy frown. He swallowed, then said, "You shouldn't have followed us."

She stared at him with an unyielding gaze and a courage she was far from feeling.

He shook his head and said almost sorrowfully, "I can't let you go, lady. The MPA would kill *me*." He shook his head again and waddled back into the kitchen.

Her shoulders sagged.

Another thirty minutes passed before the pudgy terrorist returned. He sat on the spring-punctured sofa and began playing solitaire on a coffee table marked with cigarette burns. For a while she watched the card game with an apathetic interest. When he placed Judith, the Queen of Hearts, over the Suicide King, she shuddered with an unwelcome premonition.

Being bound in such an awkward position was causing needles of pain to stab her. Gradually her arms began to lose sensation; even her fingertips were numb. She refused to cry; she was tired of crying. She just wished that whatever was going to happen, would.

Then, when Yeorgi flung open the front door, she instantly recanted. His sly expression did not bode well for her.

"Well?" Flour Sack asked, hefting himself to his feet. "What did the Oracle say to do with her?"

His mean eyes fixed on her, Yeorgi said, "The Oracle will be coming soon with his inquisition specialist, my fat friend." Slowly he bared his teeth in an unpleasant grin. "But that doesn't mean we can't enjoy ourselves while we're waiting."

Phillipa's soul shriveled into nothingness, while fear expanded in her brain like a deadly mushroom cloud. She would not—*must not* give them the satisfaction of seeing her cry.

Chapter 10

Macedonia's information network was in no way comparable to the massive, computerized files of Scotland Yard or MI6's National Crime Information Centre, although General Agamemnon had amassed a copious dossier bank, most of which dealt with both Macedonians and foreigners opposed to his tyrannical regime. Among these had been both Damon and Sigourney.

Giles was impressed that Phillipa, as well as Father Murphy, had cleverly managed to evade capture by Agamemnon's Neanderthal-looking henchman, Colonel Kopeta. In a strange way Giles felt burdened by Phillipa's extraordinary courage and spirit, the intricate nucleus of this serene, delicately boned woman.

Father Murphy and he sat hunched before microfilm readers, alone in a vaulted room in the Special
Files Department, located in the computer wing of the
National Palace's multitude of offices. They were surrounded by row after row of metal cabinets containing
newspaper articles, lab reports, photos, crime reports
and a photographic index—all stored on microfilm
reels.

Since the room was hot and stuffy, Giles had for-
saken his usual meticulousness in dress. His tie was
loosened, his Pierre Cardin jacket draped over the back
of his chair and his sleeves were rolled up. His eyes were
mapped with red lines, and his shoulders were cramped
from fatigue. An overpowering urge to get up and walk
around assailed him, but he remained glued to the
chair, forcing himself to continue scanning the monitor.

In the chair next to him, Father Murphy rubbed his
sunken eyes with the heels of his palms. The old priest
had to be hot in that heavy black cassock, Giles
thought. "The lines are all starting to run together,"
Father Murphy complained, which was unusual, because Giles couldn't remember ever hearing the old
priest grouse about anything.

After three hours of reading microfilm, Giles felt no
closer to finding Phillipa than when he had started. He
had so little information to go on: a "bilious green"
Citroën, as Father Murphy described it, and a license
plate that began with the letters ZG.

So bloody little information.

A great anger seethed in him, and only his intelligence controlled it. He shoved his fingers through his hair, then, grunting with impatience and frustration, scrolled another microfilm reel into view on the monitor.

The index of license plates had revealed that the prefix ZG applied to more than twenty-two thousand cars. A cross-check of registered late-model green Citroëns indicated none with the license plate prefix ZG. It would appear that the license plate had been stolen from another car, most likely one consigned to a dump.

"Coffee, Giles?"

He looked over his shoulder. Damon, no less, stood holding two mugs of steaming, aromatic Turkish coffee. A wide-hipped secretary hovered behind him, and he dismissed her with a brisk nod of his golden head.

"I can't believe my blurred eyes, Damon." Giles offered a weary attempt at a grateful smile. "I thought presidents had better things to do than make coffee and sharpen pencils."

The big man had craggy features that now were as inexpressive as a sphinx's. "Nothing's too menial when a life is concerned—especially the life of someone like Phillipa. Macedonia, and I, owe her...well, more than anyone could possibly guess."

He passed the other cup to Father Murphy, who said, "Bless you, Damon. Even this swamp water that passes for your national coffee is welcome this afternoon, though I suppose evening is more like it by now."

Damon's lips curved upward, though his gaze remained somber. "I would have sent out for a bottle of wine, but I didn't want to jeopardize your vows."

"Heaven forbid!" the old man said with a twinkle lighting his weary eyes.

Damon pulled a chair away from another monitor and, turning it backward, straddled it. Macedonia's leader looked out of place in his three-piece business suit, Giles thought. Slightly uncivilized. He could have been Alexander of Macedonia reincarnated. Giles suspected that Damon preferred a battlefield to the confinement of an office.

"Major Veranos," Damon began, "has alerted all our military patrols, as well as the local police forces. They're scouring Constantine and the countryside now. Broadcast bulletins have been prepared for both the television and radio stations."

"We don't have that much time," Giles replied irritably, breaking his habitual self-control. The hours of futile searching were obviously getting to him as well as Father Murphy.

"I should never have asked Phillipa to go through with this," Damon growled.

"She didn't have to accept," Father Murphy said. "Now stop flagellating yourself, my son."

"Sigourney would be furious if she knew I had let Phillipa undertake another dangerous assignment," Damon continued blackly. "Phillipa went through so damned much at Toridallos!"

"She talked about Toridallos once," Giles muttered. "But I was left with the impression that she had left out far more than she had actually included. My blood curdles when I imagine what she must have gone through."

Damon shook his head grimly. "No one who hasn't been incarcerated can even begin to imagine. A month might not seem like much, but solitary confinement in Toridallos is like a preview of hell."

Giles thought about how little he really knew about her. "Was she . . . was she tortured?"

"She only told me she was interrogated several times. She would never talk to me about it, either. Did she ever say anything to you, Father?"

The ugly priest shook his grizzled head, swallowed a sip of the thick coffee, then said, "Our Phillipa is one of those true Greek warrioresses of old."

"Phillipa is also half British, Father," Giles reminded him.

"True, and like yourselves, my sons, she is also incapable of giving her most intense fear outward expression. Whatever pressures she feels, she faces without the assistance of drink or drugs. She does what has to be done, and that is all there is to it."

Giles thought of how he had been the weaker of the two, of how he had gone to her when he had been overcome by his own private fear. She was such a strong, independent woman.

He was utterly bewitched by her lovely cultivated voice and her cool beauty, a beauty matched by her breeding and intelligence. His breath stopped at the thought of what might have happened to her, what might still happen.

He hurled the half-empty cup against the wall.

At the sound of the shattering cup, both Damon and Father Murphy glanced at the coffee-splattered wall and back to him with astonishment in their gaze.

"I've got to find her, Damon!"

Damon's eyes widened with astonishment. "So that's the way it is," he murmured.

"That's the way it is," Giles said, his cold tone forbidding any further discussion of the subject. He considered his feelings for her a private matter.

The hell of it was that he wasn't certain just what his feelings were. Or hers, for that matter. He knew she wanted him. But he wanted to be more than just someone to fill in the gap left by Damon. Or was that only his male ego wanting preeminence.

He was amazed at how much he really cared about her. Khalid had always been both impressed and disgusted by his coolness under pressure, but at the moment he certainly didn't feel cool. Cold rage—that was what he felt.

He did know that once he found her—and he *would* find her—he meant to convince her that he was more than a young man out to make his mark on an older woman.

"I suggest we go back to work on the problem of finding Phillipa," Father Murphy said, and Giles was grateful for the priest's words, which broke into his own private agony.

Damon rose from the chair. He wore the look of a condemned man facing a jury. "I have to call Sigourney and tell her what's happened."

"Not yet," Giles said. "Don't expose Phillipa's cover until there's no other option."

"You have something in mind?" Father Murphy asked, his shaggy brows drawing together.

"Possibly." Giles rubbed his jaw, which was beginning to acquire a five o'clock shadow. "It's worth a try!"

"What?" both Father Murphy and the big Macedonian asked in unison.

"I've been going at this from the wrong direction." He tightened the knot of his tie, shrugged into his jacket and left the two standing, mouths open.

Ignoring the wide-eyed stares of passersby, he loped the two blocks between the National Palace and Macedonia's criminal laboratories. After he had seen Scotland Yard's fabled laboratories, Macedonia's looked like a prep school science lab. Still, the bespectacled technician was obviously dedicated to his vocation. "I went over the evidence with microscopic care: traces of black powder and sulfuric acid, and fragments of primacord and filaments."

"Would sulfuric acid be hard to obtain? I mean, could someone buy it at a drugstore?"

"Not usually. Not in sufficient quantities, anyway. My guess is, you'd find your bomb maker working for a photo lab, since sulfuric acid is used to develop photographs. Or maybe he's a professional photographer and does his own developing."

"Oh, good!" Giles grumbled. Tracking down every photo lab and photographer in Constantine, let alone the entire country of Macedonia, could take more time than Phillipa had left. "Thanks anyway." An idea came to him. "Say, could I use your telephone?"

Without waiting for a reply Giles crossed to the telephone that sat on a counter crowded with glass test tubes, scales, rubber tubing and a World War II vintage Bunsen burner. Holding the receiver, he asked the chemist, "If I were a professional photographer, where would I place an order for sulfuric acid?"

"Well, I get my chemicals from Panayotis and Sons, a small firm outside town."

Giles made the call and, since it was after five o'clock, obtained the home telephone number of the owner—using a great deal of his charm and his persuasive Welsh voice—from the switchboard operator.

Next he called Panayotis at home, briefly explained the circumstances of the bombing, then asked, "Have there been any large-scale losses of potassium chlorate reported at your plant lately?"

"As a matter of fact," the owner said a little hesitantly, "about six weeks ago we did have a theft of sorts. My production manager on the night shift was certain one of his employees, a new man, was responsible, but couldn't prove it."

"What's the employee's name?"

"Yeorgi Kannost, but he has since quit."

"Thank you very much, Mr. Panayotis."

Giles depressed the receiver button, then rang back to the Special Files Department and got Father Murphy. "Find some way to track down the name and last known address of Yeorgi Kannost. And call me back at—" he checked the number on the telephone "—43-122."

Hands thrust in his trouser pockets, Giles paced the floor, oblivious to the mild-mannered chemist watching him with an almost clinical interest. Phillipa had been missing for more than four hours now. Anything could have happened. Giles stared absently at the telephone. He thought about ringing Damon and asking for police assistance after all, but anything out of the ordinary might alert any MPA members who witnessed it.

The telephone rang loudly, authoritatively, in the small lab, and he almost jumped. He jerked the receiver from its cradle. "Yes?"

"Found your man. Yeorgi Kannost has a criminal file that's expanding as quickly as a family tree."

"Where does he live?"

"Only a town is listed. Dalmacia, a village about a hundred kilometers north of the capital."

"Thanks, Father."

No sooner did he replace the receiver than he realized he was parked more than two blocks away. After thanking the chemist for his help, Giles didn't even wait for the elevator. He sprinted down the back stairs.

Outside he glanced around the crowded boulevard and spotted what he was seeking on the far side of the street, next to a kiosk—a parked motorbike.

He didn't even wait for a break in the heavy traffic before crossing the busy intersection but made a zig-zag dash between darting cars. Silently begging the pardon of the owner, who was doubtless one of the half dozen men lined up at the kiosk to buy a magazine or cigarettes, he climbed on the motorbike and thrust his foot down against its kick starter. At the same time he threw it into gear. With a roar the motorbike shot forward into the evening traffic.

Behind him, he heard an indistinct yell of surprise mixed with fury. "Thanks, old chap!" he shouted back.

As he headed north on Alexander Boulevard, the wind lashed his face, and he exulted in the unrestrained freedom of the ride. In the old days he had too often envied Khalid's disregard for responsibility, the way the Arab would leave the smothering duties of princedom for a wild, mad ride on his motorcycle. That was, of course, before Khalid became Baghrashi's emir and fell in love with attractive—and Irish-tempered—Alyx Langford.

Alyx, who was very much the sort of woman Giles had always been drawn to, was nothing like the cool, self-controlled Lady Phillipa—which was one reason that he couldn't understand his own passionate preoccupation with the older woman and her ineluctable mystique.

Once the thoroughfare narrowed into two lanes and the traffic thinned out, he began to strip off his jacket and tie. A little regretfully he flung the clothing, representing an outlay of nearly nineteen-hundred pounds, into the scraggly vegetation along the side of the road. Gone was the dapper British subject; in his place there was now a young man seemingly enjoying himself on a high-speed evening ride.

Enjoying himself, hell! His heart was knocking against his rib cage. How on God's green earth could he reach Phillipa in time, when he didn't even know just exactly where she was—or, and his hands went clammy on the handlebars at the thought, if she was still alive?

He slowed down the bike only when he passed through a village, and then with swearing impatience. Gradually he began to notice the tang of saltwater in the air and was able to establish on his mental map approximately where he was. At last he reached a mud brick town that a sign announced as Dalmacia—population 620.

Well, at least it wasn't a thriving metropolis—maybe three dozen streets to search. Slowly he began cycling down the main street, his gaze searching for a late-model green Citroën.

Dusk had darkened the village now, and few villagers were out to notice his passing inspection: three teenagers wearing leather jackets; a herdsman playing a reed flute; and a plump woman bearing a basket of grapes on her head. A pack of many mongrels chased after his merrily popping motorcycle.

When an aged wino lurched across the street Giles halted and asked in his badly inflected Greek, "Do you know where the Kannost house is?"

"No one lives in Dalmacia by that name," the bearded old man announced with a blast of retsina-laden breath.

Giles set off again, his motorcycle seeming inordinately loud in the sleepy village. Once he was on the unlit side streets his task became more difficult; the narrow, twisting alleyways could easily hide an automobile from view. Fortunately Dalmacia's residents didn't possess that many cars. Wooden carts with huge iron wheels seemed to be the usual mode of transportation.

He felt feverishly conscious of time ticking by swiftly. Despair was attacking his nervous system. Despite the salt breeze off the Aegean, sweat clustered in the wiry curls matting his chest.

Someone dumped refuse from an upper window, and in the action of dodging the splatter he almost missed the Citroën. It was parked on the far side of a small house on the village's outskirts.

For the first time in hours he felt a surge of hope. He shut off the motorcycle and pushed it up the dusty path that climbed toward a row of randomly spaced houses. Nearby, he half hid the machine in a straggly, wind-swept clump of stunted olive trees.

The sound of the stiff sea breeze masked his approach to the house. Its shutters were closed, but light seeped from under the weathered door. He put his ear to the wood, straining to hear over the wind, and was rewarded with the sound of voices, although he couldn't make out any distinct words. He judged that at least two men, maybe more, were inside.

And he didn't have a weapon.

There was nothing left to do but introduce himself.

Chapter 11

At Giles's knock the door was cautiously opened a crack. He seized the opportunity and kicked it open farther. The man behind it went sprawling backward. Giles's gaze had just enough time to sweep the room for Phillipa—thank God, she was there, bound and gagged but apparently unhurt!—before another man, burly and balding, flung himself at Giles's midsection.

Nimbly Giles sidestepped and drove one fist into the fleshy region just below the terrorist's solar plexus. When the man doubled over with an explosive grunt, Giles finished his task by shoving the man's chin into his own raised knee. The man's eyes flashed; then he slumped to the floor, unconscious from pain.

"Good night," Giles said, "and pleasant dreams."

Phillipa's muffled scream warned him. He spun to meet the attack of the paunchy man he had knocked down with the door—and halted abruptly. Slowly he raised his hands in deference to the lethal AK-47 pointed at him. The stocky little man's trigger finger twitched nervously, making the situation even more dangerous. At that moment Attila the Hun couldn't have looked more formidable.

"Raise your hands," the man snapped, his voice tight with barely concealed fright. "Slowly." His tongue shot out to lick anxiously at his quivering lips. "Then back up against that wall."

Giles kicked out with a thrust that sent the submachine gun spinning from the terrorist's grip. Before the man could react Giles drove the heel of his hand up under the bridge of the man's nose. The man sank to the floor, whimpering, his fat hands trying futilely to staunch the crimson fountain flooding his face.

Snatching up the AK-47, Giles ran to Phillipa. The knots binding her ankles and wrists were unnecessarily tight. "The bastards!" he cursed, noting her swollen, red flesh as he loosened the plastic cords.

When he whipped away the red mechanic's rag she began gagging. "Giles...thank God!"

He got down on his knees and caught her chin. "Are you all right?"

He was asking about more than just her physical state. There wasn't time for more questions but he wanted to know—because if she had been harmed he would kill her two captors with no more compunction than he would feel if he stepped on a roach, although the dispatching of the two would take precious time that he and Phillipa might not have.

Eyes squeezed closed, she managed to nod. Her lashes made black crescents against the lavender shadows beneath her eyes. Her face was almost the shade of the pale yellow two-piece suit she wore. "One of them . . . said that the Oracle . . . is sending an . . . interrogation team."

Behind him, Giles could hear the corpulent little man grunting and groaning. "Let's get you out of here," he told her.

He pulled her to her feet and, one arm about her waist to steady her, led her out of the house. She was shaky on her feet, but she appeared physically unharmed. She seemed so fragile that it was difficult for him to keep in mind that she had worked successfully as an undercover agent for years, when many were burned out after six months.

First he tried the Citroën, hoping the keys were inside. They weren't. So much for sending Phillipa back to Constantine on her own.

"Giles, look!"

His glance followed the direction of her wide-eyed gaze. Bobbing headlights, accompanied by the ominous purring of a car's engine, were coming up the road.

"My apologies, Phillipa." Before she could realize what he was doing, he knelt and grabbed the hem of her skirt, ripping it upward. When he rose he flashed her a reassuring smile. "Now, let's go for one wild ride, my lady."

Almost docilely, she let him half lead, half drag her through scratchy brambles over to the copse of olive trees and the motorcycle. When he helped her straddle the seat behind him, her slit skirt slid half way up her thighs. "Wrap your arms around my waist," he told her.

Obediently, her arms encircled his torso. With her firm breasts pressing against his back he felt the heat of arousal surge through him. Of all the damned times...

Just as the motorcycle roared to life, headlights spotlighted the skimpy olive trees, pinning the two of them like butterflies against night's black velvet board. A gunshot whizzed by, breaking the illusion. Phillipa cried out. Giles didn't wait another moment but shot the cycle forward into the safety of darkness.

The terrain was jarring. When the cycle crested an unexpected mound, then scrambled precariously down its bank, Phillipa's slender arms tightened even more forcefully around him.

Knowing that their only hope lay in keeping to the fields, which a car couldn't negotiate well, he headed away from civilization and its revealing lights. At first Giles thought his tactic had worked, but then the faint zigzag sweep of headlights against the scrubby vegetation ahead warned him of his error. Their pursuers were apparently driving a jeep or a Land Rover, some-

thing able to cover the same rough ground the motorcycle could.

Their options for escaping were few, and narrowing
quickly. Behind lay the village and their pursuers.
Somewhere off to the left steep cliffs plunged into the
sea. To the right stretched open fields, where their
enemies would eventually run them down. Ahead,
though, in the far distance, loomed the dark, sleeping
giant that was the Rhodope range. If they could reach
its foothills, they might reach safety.

Two miles farther on an empty irrigation ditch un-
dermined his game plan. "Hold—"

His warning shout got no further. Instantly he and
Phillipa were flung into what seemed to him like the
cosmos. The AK-47 went flying from his grip. He knew
enough from his M1 parachute training to take a rolling fall. Still, he lay stunned for several moments.
Tentatively he moved his arms and legs, then cautiously levered himself to his feet. Pain pricked a lower
rib, and his bad leg was wobbly.

"Phillipa?" He strained to listen for anything, any
sound. He heard only the distant drone of their pursuers. "Phillipa!"

He stumbled through the stygian night, trying to
discern her body amid the clumps of undergrowth. He
almost fell over the motorcycle. One look at the rear
wheel, folded in on itself, and he knew that any escape
was going to have to be made on foot.

Then, just beyond the cycle, he saw Phillipa's body.
She was curled up on herself, her eyes closed. He felt

as if a weight dropped to the pit of his stomach. He knelt and laid his fingertips along her neck, feeling for a pulse.

His touch at her throat brought a groan, at which his pent-up breath eased out of his lungs. "Phillipa, where do you hurt?"

"Everywhere."

He had to grin at that—until he heard the relentless purr of an engine again and saw the headlights leap into view. He had no time to hunt for the gun. "Can you get up, Phillipa? Out here in the open, we're ducks in a shooting gallery."

She struggled upright, then gasped. "My ankle! I must have sprained it."

He flashed her what he hoped was an encouraging smile. "Between the two of us, we make a gimpy pair."

The approaching engine sounded like a roar. "Look, can you hobble just a little farther? Over there—those low hills... With any luck we can lose those bloody bastards."

She could manage only a snail's pace. Frustrated, he scooped her up against his chest. She wrapped her arms around his neck and said against his throat, "I'm sorry, Giles."

"Just keep holding me like that," he managed to tease, "and it won't matter."

The hell it wouldn't!

He started out again, uphill—half loping, half limping. He was making quicker time, but if his bad leg collapsed, all hope would be gone.

"You're panting like an old dog," she said, straining for humor.

He couldn't help but admire her spunk, her attempt to make a joke in spite of the knife-edged danger they faced. "That's because you feel as heavy as a . . . a bag of wet cement."

The hills were becoming closer together. Negotiating them in any vehicle would be slow going now, giving him the advantage, slight though it was.

His breath was bellowing in his own ears when at last he collapsed in a ravine high in the foothills. Assuring himself that Phillipa was all right, he deserted her and, with labored breathing, climbed the ravine's side to peer out over the top.

Down below, he saw headlights moving across the brushy terrain like searchlights. He judged that he and Phillipa were reasonably safe—at least until daylight. With luck Damon would have patrols out scouring the local countryside by then.

He scrambled back down to where Phillipa sat rubbing her ankle. He dropped beside her. "Here, let me look at it." Gingerly he took hold of her small, delicate foot and felt along the bones for any swelling that might indicate a problem with the bone, rather than the ligaments or a tendon. "Doesn't seem to be anything broken."

"Ohh!" she gasped when his fingertips passed over her instep.

He grunted. "Dislocation. Take off your panty hose."

"What?"

"Do as I say. We have to bind your foot."

"Turn your head."

"Phillipa, I've seen you naked."

"That . . . that was different."

"We don't have time. Either you take them off or I will."

Eyes wary, she peeled off first one leg of her panty hose, then the other. He found her movements unbearably sensual. This was not a time to be thinking of bedding a woman. Not a woman, he corrected. This regal woman, Lady Phillipa.

"Please," she said. "Stop staring."

Heat roiled in his veins. He began unbuttoning his cuffs, then his shirt itself, and, eyes wide, she asked, "What are you doing?"

"Well, I'm not getting ready for bed."

The effort of his self-restraint made him short with her, though he didn't mean to be. For weeks now he had lived in such close contact with her without release for what he had at first cynically deemed a maddening lust. Now that he had made love to her, he found—as he had known all along he would—that it wasn't enough.

He winced as he peeled the shirt off one arm, where blood had clotted. The cool night air rushed over his bare torso as he tore the good sleeve off his shirt so he could use it as a bandage. "Somehow I managed to scratch my arm."

"Cut" was a more accurate description, but he prudently said nothing further. A strip of flesh had been gouged from the inside of his wrist up to his elbow. His system must have been flooded with adrenaline for him not to have noticed earlier.

Eyes modestly lowered, she passed him her panty hose. The fabric still held her warmth and stimulating female smell. He saw the breathless look that crept into her eyes and parted her lips. "Now let's see about bracing that ankle."

He placed the middle of his makeshift bandage under the instep of her small foot and crossed the ends at the back of her heel. As he worked he was frustratingly conscious of her: her shapely ankle; the way her calf felt in his palm, soft and supple; the scent of her fear and, yes, the scent of her own arousal.

Briskly he strapped the silky panty hose over her instep, then tied the ends. "There. If we should have to walk any farther you should be able to bear your weight."

She stared at him with a weariness that was close to the breaking point. A cool night breeze ruffled her short curls, and he felt a ridiculous urge to run his fingers through them. "We...we might have to move again?" she asked.

"Before dawn. I'm afraid you've become a wanted woman. Those goons don't plan to let you go."

She *was* a wanted woman, in more ways than one, he thought, as he gave in to the urge to touch her and lightly ran a fingertip along the ridge of her cheek, which was dark with a purpling bruise. *He* wanted her.

She flinched at his touch.

"By the light of day that bruise will look much worse. Did one of them do that to you?"

"No," she murmured, and some of the rage went out of him. "I think it must have happened when I was thrown off the motorcycle."

She was quaking with shock, and he eased her into the crook of his arm. Stroking her shoulder, he said, "It's all right, Phillipa. You're safe. It's all over."

"Safe?" she repeated, her voice quivering. "Safe is Rothingham! Safe is away from Macedonia, from Toridallos and its—its—"

She was close to crying, and he said, "Phillipa, love, tell me about Toridallos."

Sometimes, he knew, talking could be the best catharsis. In any case, talking would keep her occupied, would keep her from thinking about the horrors the immediate future might hold for them.

She tried to struggle upright, but he held her firmly against him. Then he felt her shrug, as if surrendering. "You're the only person I've ever talked to about . . . those days."

That admission made him feel a terrible sadness for her. "Then tell me more. I want to hear."

She took hold of his hand, and he could feel how cold and clammy her skin was. "There really isn't that much to tell. I wasn't actually physically tortured at

Toridallos.'' Her voice was thin, brittle, like an autumn leaf, and held a note of wary reserve.

"Tell me anyway. There's so much about you that I
don't know.''

"It was more the inhuman conditions. I had an
eight-by-ten-foot cell with a bunk and a toilet ce-
mented to the wall. I was only allowed to leave my cell
once a week to shower. I wore the same dress I was arrested in for the entire time I was there...except for my
belt. They took it away so I wouldn't attempt to hang
myself. I survived their forty-eight-hour grilling periods, but the worst was not knowing...not knowing
how long I would be there. The rest of my life, maybe?
It was the absolute hopelessness that finally came close
to breaking me.''

"You're a brave woman, Phillipa.''

"No, I'm not. I'm not,'' she cried, her reserve finally giving way, her voice anguished. "I always chose
to work undercover, you see, because I was afraid of
being exposed to harm. Sigourney...she wasn't afraid
to fight openly for Damon. Do you know, Giles, she
marched right into Toridallos to snatch him from under the guard's nose.'' Her voice rose with her emotions. "My love could never be that courag—''

His hand clamped down over her lips. She struggled
beneath him, not understanding, and he rolled atop her
to hold her thrashing body still. Her breathing was
shallow and rapid and warm against his hand. Even
knowing that their pursuers were probably nearby,

searching, he couldn't prevent his sudden arousal. It wasn't this woman's body he wanted, but this woman.

Long minutes passed before he felt it was safe to remove his hand; then he surprised even himself by replacing his hand with his mouth. Knowing it could only bring unwanted consequences, he kissed her trembling lips, anyway.

Strange. How many women he had kissed? Hundreds. And he thoroughly enjoyed the exciting, blood-rushing effect the feel of a woman's tender lips under his questing mouth had on him. But this—this feeling—staggered him. From the very first she had taken him by surprise. Twenty-four hours before, in her bedroom, he had felt as if he had been given a revelation of the exquisite joy to be found in the perfect union of two searching souls.

Regretfully he lifted his head and warned her in a low voice, "The men pursuing us...they may be nearby."

She buried her face against his bare chest, and he could feel the flushed heat of her cheeks. "Giles," she whispered, "I must be out of my mind to...to think the things I do when we could die any moment."

Her lips, brushing against one of his nipples, caused it to harden into a button of flesh. His breath rasped in his throat. She went suddenly still. Then, with a little impassioned cry, she nuzzled the hair-wreathed nipple with her nose, inhaling his scent deeply.

"Oh, Phillipa," he groaned, then anchored his hand in her short tawny curls, tugging her head back. Her

lips parted in an astonished O, she looked up at him
with as much surprise as he felt.

Danger, possibly death, surrounded them, but all he
could think of was making love to her. His fabled self-
control deserted him. He couldn't contain his hands.
Almost trembling with urgency, they loosened the first
button of her blouse, then the next, and slid inside to
cup one small but perfectly formed breast. The little
nipple peaked against his palm.

Phillipa sighed between parted lips. Her eyes glistened. "Giles...how could I have gone this long...all
my life..."

Embarrassment frayed her words, but he understood, anyway. He wanted her, too, wanted her badly.
But he couldn't risk getting caught off guard by the
terrorists. Still, her womanly softness beckoned. His
hand deserted her breast and slid up the inside of her
thigh. At his touch she stiffened. "Wait," he ordered.

Her split skirt allowed him access all the way to her
satiny panties. They were already damp. They came off
easily, and he slid down between her white thighs to
mouth her. Swiftly, he found her soft and secret place,
his tongue seeking, probing, teasing. Beneath his hands
he could feel her hips quiver with the force of the sen-
sations ravaging her body. In his delirium of passion he
knew that nothing in the world could make him stop.

When at last he lifted his head she was watching him,
her eyes heavily lidded with passion. Racking shud-
ders quaked her thighs, traveling from their epicenter

outward, and she gave little betraying moans of pleasure that had been building in her for too long.

Immediately he moved up over her, his mouth claiming hers in a silencing kiss. She opened her mouth to receive his tongue, and he had to fight against thrusting himself into her that very moment. He was as ravenous as any of the invisible animals of the night around them.

After long moments his flesh cooled and his arousal gradually diminished, though his heart still galloped like a racehorse's. He was as shaken as she by the intimate act. Great drops of perspiration clung to his forehead, just as her wonderful female scent filled his nostrils. She filled all his senses.

Above them the stars spun on their nightly course. As he tried to restore his senses to the alert, he scooped her delicate body against his. The clean, scented fragrance of her hair was disconcerting, hardly conducive to the vigilance he needed to maintain.

"Giles?"

"Yes?"

"That's never happened to me before. My husband...Aaron...never did that to me."

He had to chuckle at her modesty. "Well, love, it's about time." He started to prop himself up on one arm and winced with pain. In his frenzied lovemaking he had forgotten all about his injury.

"What is it?" she asked.

"Only this aggravating scrape on my arm. It's bleeding again."

"Let me see—my God, Giles," she whispered. "I didn't know it was so bad." She astonished him by lowering her flushed face to kiss his wound with her healing lips.

Shaken by the gesture, he caught her face between his hands and raised it, studying her features in the silvery moonlight. She was incredibly lovely. Her light brown eyes glistened with the look of a woman who was totally fulfilled, a woman who had seen and experienced life in all its variations and survived to retain her charm and strength, her wit and compassion.

Completely fascinated by her remarkable face, he failed to listen for unusual sounds and was disgusted with himself when from the bank above them, a voice growled, "Don't move!"

Three men stood there, pointing lethal looking MAC-10s, the semiautomatic guns favored by drug runners. One of them, a short, bearded man, told another, "Go down and get the Oracle. Tell him we found them." His gun still trained on Giles and Phillipa, he began to scramble down the steep bank toward them, followed by the other MPA member.

Barely moving his lips, Giles told Phillipa, "When I give you the signal, run for it."

"No, not without you!"

"Do it, Phillipa—or so help me I'll kill you myself—here and now."

Even as he spoke, he was scooping up handfuls of dirt and gravel. He flung the grit into the face of the first MPA goon.

"What—" The bearded terrorist grabbed at his eyes. The other, taken by surprise, stumbled against his companion. Off balance, the two slid down the embankment. One lost his MAC-10.

"Now, Phillipa!" Giles yelled at the same instant. "Get out of here!"

She hesitated, saw his unyielding expression and turned to run, though she could manage little more than a quick hobble. He didn't wait to see if she made it out of the ravine to safety. He made a base-sliding dive for the rolling, clattering semiautomatic, only to have to wrestle for ownership with the bearded man.

Out of the corner of his eye he saw the other terrorist approaching. With a herculean effort Giles yanked the gun loose from the bearded man's grasp and, in the same movement, swung it sideways into the pit of the second man's stomach. The man doubled over, and Giles jerked the muzzle upward, holding the gun trained on both men. "Back off—slowly!"

"Not so fast," a voice said from behind him. Before he could spin around, something metallic clipped him on the skull. With the ravine spinning around him like a top, he collapsed on his knees.

The man nearest Giles called to one of the men at the top of the embankment, "What do we do with him?"

Giles shook his head, trying to clear the blinding dizziness, and pain drove through his brain like a silver spike. Tears of pain burst from his eyes.

"He knows too much. Shoot him. And find the woman. She can't have gone far. Take care of her, too."

The voice was a new one, Giles thought, but its authoritative tone told him that it almost certainly belonged to the Oracle of Delphi. A roaring filled his head. At first he thought it was from the blow, but in the next second he realized he was hearing a car engine. His tear-blurred gaze saw headlights flash over the ravine's rim. Men scattered, diving from the path of the speeding vehicle.

Not quite believing his eyes, Giles watched as a jeep crested the ravine and hurtled down the slope toward him. At the last minute it swerved away, and Phillipa yelled out, "Get in!"

Chapter 12

Phillipa was to be locked away from the world with Giles, ordered into hiding by Damon until the terrorists could be tracked down.

She stood in the doorway and glanced around the apartment that had once given the shelter of anonymity to Damon and Sigourney. The place was shabby, a cluster of three little rooms tucked away on a meandering back street in one of the ghettos of Constantine's Old Town. The street sounds were loud and distracting, and Phillipa crossed the main room to close the cracked window. The apartment had been built above a leather shop, and the odor of soft leather and the faint smell of the lime solution used for tanning lingered inside.

She ran a finger down one peeling wall, wondering how long this interlude, which it seemed God had chosen to grant her in life's later years, would last. Was her allotment of joy to be measured in hours, or days, perhaps even weeks? So much had happened to change her within the past forty-eight hours.

Though she was forty-six, her body had been largely a mystery to her. Suddenly, almost overnight, she was going through the metamorphosis that a butterfly, emerging from its chrysalis, takes weeks to achieve. But then, she thought reflectively, perhaps her metamorphosis had taken forty-six years to achieve.

All her thoughts centered on her struggle to understand the desire growing within her, filling her. She felt that at any moment she might shut her eyes and fall off a precipice. Giles had awakened her sexuality, and she reveled in it, daring to dream of doing things no proper lady dared to dream of. She was involved in a monumental process of self-discovery. Gradually Giles was battering down her inhibitions. With him, she felt no shame.

Behind her, Giles closed the door. Since escaping the Oracle and his MPA terrorists, she and Giles had had little chance to talk to each other. Father Murphy's presence, as he drove them to the apartment in his usual erratic fashion, had only served to intensify the silence that had stretched like a frayed rubber band between them.

Now she and Giles were alone.

He crossed the small room to her and kissed her neck, then locked his arms around her, so that they crossed in front of her rib cage. Gently, tenderly, he caressed her breasts. "I know what you want," he said, affirming her desire. In traitorous response her nipples hardened against the satiny material of her blouse.

"I know your ivory body and how it reacts to my hands. But I don't know *you*, Phillipa. I don't know your mind. I don't know all the joys and hurts and hopes that went into making you the complex woman you are."

She twisted in his embrace to face him. Surely the powerful wave of desire washing through her must show in her face. She felt like a greedy, newly hatched nestling, her mouth always open, her capacity endless.

"You only need to know that I'm grateful for this idyll, Giles. Up until two days ago, my body wasn't anything other than a vessel for my soul and a source of my husband's pleasure." She turned away from him, unwilling to let him see her soul in her eyes.

"But not your own pleasure?" He moved his hand downward past the plateau of her stomach to cup the slight mound at the apex of her legs. "You're so beautiful," he whispered against her ear. "Relax, love, and rest your head against my shoulder."

All her concentration was focused on the miraculous touch of his hand until the whole world seemed to tremble, until the entire cosmos threatened to end in a single splintering moment of unbearable pleasure.

She knew she cried out, but she didn't hear herself. When her lover turned her in his arms to face him, she shook with a joy so intense that, looking into his blue eyes, she knew she had astonished not only herself but him.

"The labs have run a fingerprint check on the jeep," Father Murphy told Phillipa and Giles, while he chopped the celery he had brought, along with other groceries, from the marketplace in Old Town.

She had insisted that the priest stay for lunch, perhaps because she wasn't quite ready to deal with her newfound sensuality. She welcomed the presence of a third party so that she was free to step back and assess the man who had entered her fantasies and changed them to realities.

Giles was attentive in the way of a young man already wise about women, a man who seemed to sense that all the tenderness he would ever learn derived from this one woman. From Phillipa herself. The idea was a source of amazement to her.

"What did they find?" he asked the priest as he poured three glassfuls of retsina.

Phillipa yearned to trace the strong line of his mouth, to stroke his hair-matted arms and broad chest. He looked more attractive than ever in the jeans and cream-colored chambray shirt Father Murphy had procured for him. The priest had also managed to purchase a cotton caftan and delicately fashioned sandals for her.

"The jeep, naturally, is stolen. Only one set of fingerprints turned up. They belonged to a man by the name of Yeorgi Kannost." He glanced pointedly at Giles. "The same one who formerly worked at Panayotis."

"That's the name of one of the men who held me captive!" Phillipa said.

"Research into his past shows him to be a former inmate of Toridallos," the old priest said, taking a noisy bite of celery. "He escaped, along with hundreds of others, during the overthrow of Agamemnon."

A shudder of old fear rattled up her spine, and Giles told her quietly, reassuringly, "It's over, love."

"If anyone can track the man down, Veranos can," Father Murphy said.

"Who knows we're here?" Giles asked, changing the subject.

"Only myself and Damon. Well, my children, are we going to drink the wine?"

Giles handed each of them a chipped glass and added, smiling, "To health and long life."

Father Murphy raised his own glass to join in the toast, but she could feel his shrewd gaze moving from her to Giles, speculating about the nature of the relationship that had developed between them. Crimson flooded her cheeks, and she turned away and went back to chopping onions for a simple salad.

"Let me help," Giles said, and rolling up his cuffs, he began washing his hands in the cracked porcelain sink. He circled her slowly, she the center, he the orbit. Excitement pulsed in her. Her joy might be short-lived, but right now it perked in her blood and crackled in her brain. The night would be too long in coming.

While Giles tore up lettuce into a pottery bowl, Father Murphy chatted jovially as he finished dicing the celery. She knew the priest was trying to alleviate the high-voltage tension and barely concealed restraint his presence had created.

Over lunch all three of them conspired to keep the conversation light, as if by tacit consent, and they all laughed readily.

"Father," Giles asked, "did you always want to be a priest?"

"Heavens, no, my son. Until I was twenty I dreamed of being a movie star."

Giles flashed Phillipa a covert, questioning glance, and she shrugged imperceptibly, not certain whether the priest was joking with them or steadfastly serious.

"What happened to change your mind?" Giles asked.

The priest's jowls shook with silent mirth. "The first casting director I was sent to told me outright that the only film he would ever cast me in would be a horror picture."

"You're making all that up, you lovable old coot!" she accused.

"Old?" he chuckled. "Why, Phillipa, my child, I take my cue from the movies. Instead of old age, I call my life *Youth—Part III.*"

She and Giles laughed along with the priest, but in the back of her mind a voice whispered, "There it is again—the unavoidable issue of age."

In the tiny bedroom, with its dust-streaked windows, Giles made love to Phillipa slowly, as if memorizing each part of her to be recalled later. She had to fight herself to keep from letting go. He leaned over her, removing her caftan, kissing her knees, stroking her breasts. Ashamed of her less than perfect body, she tried to draw the sheet over herself.

"Don't, love." His expression became serious, his dark blond brows meeting over the strong line of his nose. "You're a grown woman with a beautiful body and a wealth of experience. I would count it an enormous loss if you denied both of us all that you are."

She turned her face up to his, fitting her mouth to his, meeting his tongue with hers. When he put his hand between her legs she couldn't believe how ready she was after his infinitely patient and tender ministrations.

She remembered how, through the years, she would freeze just before making love with Aaron, so that it was painful for her. Always afterward feelings of her inadequacy lingered, though Aaron never alluded to any possible discontent with their love life.

Giles took her hand and guided it down the plunge of crisp stomach hair. She wrapped her hand around him and beneath her sensitive fingers she felt him hard and throbbing. "See the power you have over me, love?"

The stark realization that she alone was responsible for his powerfully aroused state was overwhelming. Womanhood! Why had she waited so long to discover her full potential?

He moved up over her, and they became one...legs, arms, mouths, breasts, hard, soft, wet, hot. At first she couldn't tell if he was hurting her or pleasuring her to madness. All she knew was that she would never have enough of him. Then the feeling became unbelievably, unbearably good. Her passion surrounded his passion. Their desires were matched, their flesh momentarily one flesh.

When he achieved release deep inside her, she exulted in his exultation. Afterward he lay beside her, watching her face in the soft light of a lamp that he had insisted on leaving lit. He smelled of youth, she thought, and of sweat and man, sweet, like clover.

Almost wonderingly he fingered her tousled curls. "When I lay awake at night in your villa, I used to think about you, alone, in your room. I wanted you badly, but my curiosity often overcame my wanting. I tried to imagine what your life had been like before Agamemnon came to power."

"And what did you imagine?"

"I imagined charity organizations, dinners, the opera, jet-setting across the Continent. Sometimes I would wonder if our paths had crossed in London and we'd never known it. Then I realized how awful your life must have become during Agamemnon's regime—a life of pain and secret that you led in behalf of Macedonia. The false smiles and swiftly fabricated stories, and always the strained nerves."

She caught his marvelous, supple fingers and kissed them one by one. "That other life I led made the pain of Aaron's death and Macedonia's suppression more bearable."

When she awoke the next morning her feelings were directed only at preserving the beauty of the night before, retaining the sensation, holding on to the ecstasy that she now knew was her feminine birthright. And because this was the first time she had experienced such love, she awoke to an awful sense of its mortality.

In the faint light of dawn she studied Giles's superb body, not surreptitiously or fleetingly, but absorbing his image at that wondrous moment to remember it forever.

What she and Giles shared...it would have to end when they left the apartment. She knew that, intellectually, at least.

Giles was still young. She would be cheating him of some of the best years of his life if she let their relationship continue as it was now. He deserved a family, children. One of their first conversations had dealt with his strong desire to carry on his Welsh bloodline.

Children, something she could never give him.

If she loved him, she would set him free.

Over the next few days they talked often, mostly of inconsequential things. Of course, the word love was never mentioned by either of them. Only the very old, she thought, and the very young, dared to use that word.

Sometimes they held late-night discussions on mortality and human need and political versus moral responsibility; other times they joked about silly things, and she would laugh until there was no longer a Macedonia or terrorists or an age difference, until the tears that filled her eyes were not for the long years of emptiness and loneliness to come, but simply for joy and its concomitant possibility: love.

She was washing the chipped plates and glasses. Beside her, Giles dried. He wore only jeans, his broad chest rising above the narrow waist like a sleek slab of Carrera marble. It was almost impossible for her to rivet her attention on the dinner dishes.

"I try to imagine you as a teenager," she said, smiling as she swirled the warm sudsy water over a cracked saucer. "With all your arrogance, you must have been the object of every Welsh maiden's dreams."

A wry smile lifted the corners of his mouth. "Hardly. I might have been crammed with hormones and ambition, but my skin was coated with dirt and coal dust, and there were permanent half moons of black under my nails. All the men—except the very wealthy—were covered with coal dust. I swore that if I ever escaped the mines, I'd never be dirty again."

That, she thought, explained his immaculateness—and the way he dressed.

"Everyone who worked the mines was stooped. For all one of our Welsh maidens knew, I could have been six or sixty. Sometimes I felt like sixty."

"Perhaps that's what makes you seem so much more mature than thirty-two."

He looped his dish towel around her waist and pulled her against his taut body. Looking down at her, he said, "Age has nothing to do with the attraction between a man and a woman, Phillipa. You make me feel things I didn't know had anything to do with a male-female relationship."

"And none of the other women—girls your age," she amended, "ever did?"

"Some of them... well, you couldn't call them overliberated.... They were just born sharks. Others, it was like talking to beautiful dolls. There was no real chemistry. Nothing like what I'm feeling now," he teased, nuzzling her neck.

Surprising her, he lapped his hands around her waist and hoisted her onto the counter. "What are you doing?" she laughed.

His expression altered, a slight flaring of the nostrils, a pressing together of the lips, as if to contain his excitement, and the setting of the jaw that reminded her of his lone-wolf nature and the way he was sufficient unto himself.

"I am going to make love to you," he said quietly, determinedly.

"Here? On the kitchen counter?"

He lifted a brow and asked mildly, "Why not?"

She couldn't protest, because she was suddenly choked with raw desire, with the tidal waves of a strange emotion.

He wedged himself between her legs and, button by button, loosened her caftan, pushing it aside to bare her breasts. When he took her nipples in his fingers she went breathless with the supreme pleasure that rushed through her veins. His hands were expertly at work, his touch both tender and sure.

She was wet, excited. A heat that was growing to be familiar spread down her thighs. She was like a child, she thought abstractedly—greedy for sensation, greedy for pleasure, greedy for all of life that would too soon be over for her.

Recklessly, boldly, she leaned forward and unzipped his jeans. He was swollen and throbbing in her fingers. His hands cupped her hips, and he pulled her forward, lifting her up, impaling her on the object of her worship. Her body was ablaze.

Beneath her hands, his biceps were rigid with the effort of slowly lifting and lowering her onto him. Feeling herself in flames, she threw her head back, eyes closed, feeling herself sheathing him.

His rapid breathing lifted his chest, its mat of hair damp with perspiration. Her fingers traced the aureolae of his nipples, and he gasped, "If you don't stop, Phillipa, it'll be over before I've even begun!"

She didn't want to stop. She wanted more. She craved the taste and the musky smell of him, needing more intimacy than she had experienced. "Then I'll do this," she told him with a wicked smile and began kissing his ear.

"That's quite enough!" he choked, turning his head.

Riding his magnificent body, she felt like a wild Valkyrie. She hardly recognized herself anymore. She did know that she wanted this moment to last, wanted to store it in the pleasure cells of her brain, to bring forward when she was alone in the years to come. Closing her eyes tightly, she squeezed back the climactic tide of pleasure that would too quickly ebb. But all her efforts were in vain. She was unable to stem the explosion within her.

When it was over he touched her cheek and said, almost wonderingly, "You're crying. Why?"

"It was so good!" Such joy had to be as short-lived, she knew, as the fleeting moments in which their bodies merged together, moving in tandem to a universe beyond time, before returning inevitably to earth.

As it had for Damon and Sigourney, the small, bare apartment became a place of beauty to Phillipa, where she learned the exquisite joy of love—and there was no denying that she had fallen in love with Giles. Every so often she thought about confessing to him the way that her growing love for him had already replaced any desire to return to England. But she knew instinctively that such a confession would be foolhardy. Giles was still young, and he still had his own destiny to fulfill. In no way could she be a part of it. Their paths should never have crossed—but they had. Oh, cruel fate!

One night, when they had been locked away from the world for four days, they lay talking about Macedonia and its bleak situation with the MPA terrorists. "I'd know the Oracle's voice if I ever heard it again," Giles said.

"Then you don't think Father Murphy is our traitor?"

He shook his head. "I don't know. I don't think so. I hope not. At least I'm sure he's not the Oracle. Perhaps he's—"

Suddenly the lights went out, not just in the bedroom, but all over that part of the ghetto. The room was as dark as a cave. He sat bolt upright. "Phillipa!"

She put her hand on his shoulder. "I'll find candles. I'm sure there must be some here somewhere."

In the dark, his hand clamped down on her thigh. His palm was sweaty. His voice was rough, strangled. "No. Stay with me."

At the urgency in his voice she said, "The lights will come on soon."

She doubted if she could have pulled away from the hold he had on her leg even if she had wanted to. She rolled back onto her side and put her hand on his shoulder. His muscles were knotted with tension. "Giles, will you lie down beside me again?"

Gone were his lithe, graceful movements. His body was taut and strained, damp with perspiration, as he reclined next to her.

She pulled him into her arms and murmured in conversational tones, "This happens every so often here in the ghetto. These people are so set in their ways that it's difficult to get them to update their obsolete local utility equipment."

Why was she telling him all this? As Damon's special project administrator, he was no doubt already familiar with these problems. "Giles, please explain to me why you hate the darkness."

Silence answered her, and she prompted anxiously, "Were you locked in a closet as a child, or something like that?" She had to make him talk to her. "It's the mines isn't it?" She should have known at once.

He stiffened, moving mere millimeters away, although she still cradled him. In the night his voice was low and terse, and she sensed that he was forcing the words from his throat, that he would have talked about anything if it would have taken his mind off the darkness.

"My older brothers and my father and his father...they disemboweled the mountain for its coal with primitive hand tools. They formed underground cathedrals, separated by huge pillars of unmined rock. It's difficult to believe that such work was done by candlelight."

"But you told me that you had worked there, too."

"Yes," he gritted, "One by one the men of my family died off. They were victims of rockfalls, silicosis and *Ffestiniog fever.*"

"What's that?"

"It's like typhoid fever. My father and brothers carved their own awesome memorials inside those mountains."

"Go on."

His strong fingers dug into her flesh. "Mother didn't want me to work the mines. I was her baby. The last of her children, the last of her sons. But the lack of money made it necessary that I also go underground. We were poor, you see."

"Yes, I know," she said, covering her anxiety with a serenity she was far from feeling. "The plight of the miners was one of my father's concerns as a member of parliament. How old were you?"

"Eight. A candle was our only light. We'd climb up the slate face, eighty feet sometimes. We'd hang there by a chain wrapped around one leg while we drilled holes for blasting powder. I mightn't have been so brave those first few days if there had been enough light for me to see how high I was. Then, when I did get a glimpse, I became absolutely terrified of falling as well as the darkness."

Listening to the man she loved, she thought that, yes, he was human, he was capable of fear—just as he was capable of terrible violence. She had witnessed it the night he'd rescued her. She pried his clenched hand from hers and tenderly kissed his palm. "I understand," she murmured against his fingers. "But I'm here with you now, and whenever you want me, my love."

He turned to her, taking her into his arms, crushing her against his hot, damp body, and buried his mouth on hers. Even as she gave herself up to the urgency of his kiss, she thought, I, too, have a fear, a new fear, my greatest fear: that to be as happy as I am is impossible. It cannot last, not in this world.

But there was no other world that she wanted. Not any world to come, or any world that was past.

Chapter 13

Within the crumbling walls of Old Town, Phillipa deemed it safe to make the purchases necessary for another few days of hiding—items such as toothpaste and shampoo that Father Murphy had neglected earlier that morning when delivering groceries and a sheaf of state papers marked for Giles's attention.

"Damon thought working on that hydroelectric project would keep you occupied," Father Murphy had said, his eyes twinkling within their sunken sockets.

"I have enough to occupy me," Giles had retorted, directing a raffish grin at her.

The old priest had assured them that Major Veranos felt it would only be a matter of a few more days before the wanted bulletins and posters brought Yeorgi Kannost—and the Oracle—out of the cold.

She walked as briskly as possible through the crowded maze of booths and stalls and shops that Sigourney had once said reminded her of an Arab souk. With Giles in the apartment, absorbed in the dam project, Phillipa didn't need to hurry, but she was anxious to get back, anyway. Every moment away from him was wasted, never to be recalled . . . and, oh there was such short time left to her.

Because this was the first time she had experienced such love, she realized that what was so beautiful also had to be fragile and precious; she felt, with a conviction that left no room for the variable of hope, that there simply could be no meaning to her life without Giles.

She tried to be realistic and rational about the situation, but at her age losing the one she loved would be like death.

More than anything she dreaded the moment when Father Murphy would show up and announce that the Oracle and Yeorgi had been apprehended. Giles's task would be finished. He would leave for Wales for the rest of his life.

Phillipa wended through the marketplace's exotic press of people: Greek women in white aprons and merino stockings; Arabs in red tarbooshes; Hassidic Jews in black-brimmed beaver hats and side curls; and Turks in fezzes sporting horse tails. Within the walled section of Constantine the black market thrived, and she was able to make her purchases quickly and cheaply without wasting undue time on the ancient art of bargaining.

In her mind's eye she pictured Giles at the dining room table, his golden head propped on one palm as he penciled through the papers left by Father Murphy. A wistful smile curved the ends of her lips as she handed over a handful of drachmas in payment for a bottle of shampoo.

With feverish steps she made her way back to the shabby little apartment—and Giles. At Arcadia she had resisted his dominating manner. She had been as fiercely independent as he. Here, in the Old Town apartment, no struggle for supremacy existed between them. Where change was required, she was willing to adjust, because she knew that if a person really cared about someone, that person did what was necessary—or that was the end.

She ignored her fear of the inevitable termination of their relationship and, in place of her fear, learned to embrace the moment, to celebrate the joy of freedom from all her old inhibitions, a freedom that she had previously found so hard to accept as her birthright. She knew she would never love again the way she loved Giles.

When she entered their apartment he was still laboring over his paperwork, his pencil flying furiously. Sunlight pouring through the window illuminated his hard, ascetic features, intense with preoccupation. For a moment she let her hungry eyes caress his fine young body.

Rather than disturb him, she would have passed on by the table, but he forestalled her, wrapping an arm around her waist. His eyes, their color deepened to ultramarine, roamed over her face hungrily. She wanted desperately to ask, *Do you love me?* but her aristocratic pride wouldn't let her.

"You were gone a long time," he said, nuzzling the valley between her breasts. "Too long. I worried about you . . . and wanted you."

"Again?" she teased, but she was pleased—and terribly excited. Incredible how just a look from him was able to do that to her.

"Again."

Laughing, she sidestepped out of his embrace. "Not until after I prepare lunch, you lecherous Welshman!"

She went to the kitchen and began unpacking her purchases, when inexplicably, uneasiness began to chill her. Something dangerous and ugly had entered her psychic domain.

In the next instant the shattering of glass was like thunder in her ears. Then the windowless kitchen was lit by a searing white glare. A tremendous explosion ripped through the apartment. The blast sent her reeling against the kitchen's back wall.

For a long moment she lay slumped there, half-stunned. Her eardrums ached from the blow, and her breath had been punched from her lungs. Plaster from the ceiling was falling on her as she hauled herself up by the nearby countertop. Other sounds reached through the ringing in her ears: the tinkle of falling shards of glass; the cracking of broken furniture; and the thud of still-falling plaster.

Then a terrible fear struck her heart, squeezing like the talons of a vulture. "Giles!" she screamed, and rushed into the other room.

A soft white cloud of phosphorus smoke billowed across the floor like a summer fog and drifted upward. Small flames licked avidly along what was left of the sofa. The bedroom door leaned drunkenly on one hinge.

Half-blinded by tears and smoke, she groped through the debris that had once been furniture and walls. A yawning hole gaped in the floor. The floury taste of plaster dust filled her mouth, and the bitter stench of burned explosive assailed her nostrils.

With a strength that later surprised her, she rapidly shoved away the living room door where it lay propped on one end of the collapsed table—all that was left of the table, in fact. Beneath, she found only the fragmented parts of a chair.

"Giles!" she cried again, her anguish pitching her voice high. Scalding tears coursed down her cheeks.

Finally she discovered him flung against one wall, like a toy tossed away by a child in a tantrum. A great coldness filled her chest. She knelt beside him and touched his jaw. "Giles!" she begged, "are you all right? Please, dear God, be all right!"

He groaned and lifted his head. Blood, as rich and red as wine, ran down over his eyes. She was consumed by a terrible rage. "Those murderous bastards! Damn them!"

The ambulance hurtled through Constantine's busy streets. The siren shrieked a dirge in Phillipa's ears. *She* felt like shrieking, but she clamped a bell jar of calmness over her emotions as she watched a paramedic take Giles's vital signs, first his pulse, then his blood pressure.

After the paramedic finished and quickly jotted down the cold statistics, he efficiently swabbed the inside of Giles's arm, then inserted an IV needle. Phillipa swayed, feeling sweat drip down her back and legs.

From a bottle a solution flowed through a tube into Giles's veins. The paramedic, looking like a puzzled owl, glanced up at the bottle and frowned. "We're getting uneven flow. Take it off the hook, will you? Hold it directly over the patient. High."

Phillipa felt a buzzing in her head, and the young man snapped, "Don't get dizzy!"

She took a deep, steadying breath, rose and took the jar from the hook, as instructed. Once again she swayed, but this time from the motion of the ambulance as it careened around a corner. Paralyzed with dread, she felt like one of those Grecian women raising their jars, immortalized as marble statues. Abstractedly she watched the solution flow from the bottle and into Giles.

Dear God, please, please, let him live. Let him be all right! she prayed silently.

Her love for him had brought about this terrible fear of his mortality, of the fragility of human life in an eternity of death and birth. His beauty and his arrogance and his strength were ephemeral, like everything else that lived in the world. The fact that life and love could not last made her want to kneel at once at his side and clutch him to her breast.

At the starkly modern Mount Athos Hospital, interns and nurses took over with an efficiency that left her standing helplessly, watching as they wheeled Giles away on a bed. She refused to be checked over by an intern on duty. "I'm all right."

"Your hand is bleeding," the doctor pointed out mildly.

She must have cut it when she was sifting through the debris, searching for Giles. "It's nothing. A bandage will do."

Distractedly she submitted to being bandaged and answered the probing questions of a matronly nurse. After that, for what seemed like an eternity, she sat in an antiseptic-smelling waiting room, holding her private, agonizing vigil. Her eyes felt bruised from sleeplessness.

At some point during the night Father Murphy joined her, though she couldn't remember giving the officious admittance clerk the priest's name. "Damon and Sigourney are on their way, my child."

She buried her face against his chest. "Oh, Father, Giles mustn't die!"

The priest patted her back. "Of course he mustn't. A few prayers are in order. They'll keep us occupied—and the Lord, as well."

Perhaps an hour later—or maybe more, Phillipa wasn't certain—Damon and Sigourney arrived. It was almost dawn, and she and Father Murphy were sitting, drinking stale coffee from Styrofoam cups. She and the old priest rose stiffly from the uncomfortably hard chairs to greet the others. She felt as if she had aged ten years during the past twelve hours.

Even there, at the hospital, Damon's life wasn't his own. Three well-dressed but not otherwise ostentatious men accompanied him. Only the slight bulges beneath their jackets and the small receivers secured in their ears identified them as members of Macedonia's secret service, bodyguards of the president.

Sigourney hugged Phillipa to her. The other woman hadn't even taken the time to apply makeup, yet somehow, Phillipa thought admiringly, Sigourney still managed to look youthful and fresh. "We came as soon as we heard! Are you all right, Phillipa?"

"Yes, fine." She brushed the back of her hand across her forehead. "Thank you for coming. Friends like you and Damon and Father Murphy are..." She paused, trying to keep her voice from cracking. "I need your friendship and your prayers very much right now."

While Sigourney conversed quietly with Father Murphy, Damon drew Phillipa aside and asked, "Did you tell anyone where you and Giles were hiding?"

She shook her head slowly, still feeling the after-shock of the thunderous explosion pulsing within. "No, absolutely not. Only you and—" Her startled gaze flew up to meet his grim one. "Surely you don't think Father Murphy could have..."

"I don't know what to think."

A doctor, still wearing a green surgical cap and with his mask hanging around his neck like a bandit's bandana, entered the waiting room. "Lady Phillipa?" he asked.

Phillipa whirled expectantly. Her heart thudded painfully against her rib cage. "Yes? I am she."

"I'm Dr. Nicolaidis, chief surgeon at Mount Athos." He recognized Damon and shook his hand, saying respectfully, "Mr. President."

Abstractedly she noted that the surgeon's fingers were as delicate as a young girl's. "Giles...?" she asked the doctor. "Will he live?"

"Most certainly."

She should have felt relief, but there was something unrelieved in the set of the surgeon's mouth. "Is he...?" she began to ask, feeling her heart thudding like a jackhammer. "Is Giles going to be all right?"

He spoke with an impersonal candor that chilled her. "A tiny steel fragment, probably from the grenade, entered the skull through the left temple and severed a large vein—which accounts for the profuse bleeding, Lady Phillipa. We were able to remove the fragment with relatively little difficulty."

"But?" she breathed, feeling the band of cold around her rib cage.

The surgeon's mouth tightened, and he looked away from her anguished face. "The corneas of his eyes were burned by the explosion. They will be a mass of scar tissue. As a result, he is blind."

She sagged, and only Damon's quick hands supporting her weight kept her upright. "I'm all right," she murmured, drawing a steady breath.

"Is this condition permanent?" Father Murphy asked the surgeon. "What about corneal transplants?"

The surgeon rubbed his eyes with his thumb and forefinger, then looked at the four expectant faces. "If the corneas only were burned, then transplants might work. But it appears that the retinas, behind the corneas, don't respond to light, indicating that they are detached. He has no recognition of shape and color, of light or darkness." He paused, then said with a crisp and brutal honesty, "Giles Hayes-David has been permanently and totally blinded in both eyes."

Sigourney put a consoling arm around Phillipa's waist, and Phillipa had never been so grateful for the husband and wife who stood supportively on either side of her. All she could think of was Giles's terror of the dark—and how now he was consigned to darkness for life. "Have you told him yet, Dr. Nicolaidis?" Sigourney asked.

"No. I thought it would be best if someone near to him did that."

"Can I go to him now?" Phillipa asked.

"He is lightly sedated, but awake."

Giles lay on a high bed beside the curtained window. In contrast to the soft cotton dressing that thickly covered both his eyes, the pure lines of his face looked carved from golden marble. At the quiet swishing of the door closing, his head turned toward her with anesthetic-clumsy slowness.

"Giles." Her voice was barely a whisper. She took his hand and squeezed it between hers.

"Phillipa!" he mumbled. "Thank God you're alive! Are you all right?"

"I'm fine, my love." She bent to kiss his lips. They were chilled, and smelled of anesthetic. "Thank God *you're* alive."

"I must have a concussion of sorts."

"Giles, there's something I have to tell—"

"I'm finished with hiding, Phillipa. As soon as I'm discharged, I'm going to hunt down those swine if I have to search every household in Macedonia!"

"Giles."

At the warning tone in her voice, he went absolutely still, so still that it seemed he didn't even breathe. After a moment he asked, "What is it?"

She knew he wasn't the sort of man who would want to be indulged. She said bluntly, "Your eyes were burned by the explosion. You've been blinded... for life."

His hand in hers was the only indication he had heard her. It spasmed convulsively like a wounded thing, then went still.

Say something! she thought wildly. Yell! Vent your rage at such an injustice. Those marvelous blue eyes...their color paled, clouded by scar tissue.

At last he said, "I see." Then, with a twisted grin, he said, "Forgive the pun."

Tears ran unchecked over her cheeks, and she couldn't speak.

"Please...I need to think, Phillipa. And I'm very drowsy."

"I understand," she whispered hoarsely. "I'll be outside."

Damon was waiting for her in the hallway. He motioned away two of the three bodyguards who had accompanied him. Odd, she thought, how Damon was nothing more to her now than a very, very dear friend. With him she had shared the horrors of Toridallos and the hopes for Macedonian freedom.

"I left Sigourney with Father Murphy. I wanted to talk to you alone, Phillipa. The MPA know that you can identify at least one of them, and for all they know Giles could identify the voice of the Oracle. Once the MPA learn you and Giles are still alive, they won't stop until you're both lying on a slab in the morgue."

With a shiver she rubbed her goose-fleshed arms. "I won't let them kill him, Damon. I had nothing until he came into my life."

"Listen to me, Phillipa." He gripped her arms. "I talked to Dr. Nicolaidis. He says that the temple wound is external, that Giles can be discharged as early as the day after tomorrow, if he takes it very easy. Until then, guards will be posted here to protect you two. With Giles registered here under his own name, though, I doubt there will be any trouble. Come the day after tomorrow, I want you both out of here, out of Constantine."

She sighed and rubbed her temples. Her head was pounding. "Where can we go that they can't track us down? I'm beginning to think it's impossible to elude this Oracle of Delphi."

"No, it isn't! There is a place where he will never think to look for you two. Now, do what I say. In two days a rented car will be waiting in the hospital parking lot. I'll get word to you of the model, and where it's parked.

"I want you to take Giles and drive to the St. Nicolas Monastery. Only a few Orthodox monks still reside there to attend to the needs of the handful of pilgrims who visit each year. They can care for you until the Oracle is hunted down."

The European monasteries were little republics that ruled themselves. In medieval times they were places to find serenity and quiet, as well as safety from marauding bandits. Now the monasteries catered mostly to the wealthy.

Far away from the cares of the rest of humanity, the St. Nicolas Monastery towered high above the Aegean Sea at the end of a thirty-five-mile-long peninsula in southeastern Macedonia. Founded near the village of Karpeta in the mid-thirteenth century, the Eastern Orthodox monastery stood like a fortress, its massive, crenellated walls part of the sheer cliff. Within the sanctuary-keep above the sea, pious men retreated from the world, bending their necks to the yoke of obedience and, through self-denial and punctilious repetition of ritual, following unquestioningly an ordained path to salvation.

Giles was Phillipa's salvation. He was what made her world spin. He had opened her to life in so many ways; he had returned to her the gift of her senses. She could feel only an immense joy that he was alive, that he was beside her as she drove the rented Volvo up the jolting road that climbed the windswept promontory where the monastery perched like a protective eagle.

"I suppose I should feel honored," she told him, trying to keep the conversation light. "No female has been allowed to set foot in St. Nicolas for a thousand years."

"A concession obtained by our persuasive Damon?"

"No small feat, I imagine."

Giles's handsome head canted as he listened. His eyes were still covered by cotton pads and dressings that needed to be changed daily for another week. "I can hear—and smell—the sea. I never thought of it as hissing.''

"Yes, this road runs parallel to the cliff's edge.''

She had to wonder if the darkness of being blind was as terrifying to Giles as the darkness of the night. He seemed to have stoically accepted his blindness, but she realized that it was still too soon to see how he would adjust. Only time would reveal just how well he would do, but she meant to be there for him when he needed her.

Father Stavroniketa, his beard as black as his robe and cylindrical hat, was the *archontaris*, or guestmaster, of the monastery. Like Father Murphy, he radiated inner peace and joy as he offered her and Giles the ritual brandy, coffee, gummy sweet *loukoumi*, and water, then showed them to a neat, two-story stone guesthouse with a flower-lined balcony overlooking the wave-washed rocks below.

"People come to us troubled,'' Father Stavroniketa said, standing in the center of the main room, which had a wide fireplace and hand-woven woolen rugs scattered over the stone floors to ward off the chill from the sea. The rugs would have to go, she thought, already establishing herself as Giles's eyes.

"A month or so in the monastery brings peace,'' Father Stavroniketa continued, his gentle smile revealing a gold tooth. "The guests leave, refreshed and renewed.''

She had already been renewed—by Giles. Now it was her turn to give to him.

"You two will be our only guests for a while," the monk was saying, "and if there is anything you may need, there are five of us here to make your retreat a restful one."

Here at St. Nicolas, she thought, we will be safe. Here names were never asked, never used. Nor did the monks ask what a person did, where he came from, whether he believed, why he was there. Moreover, the vast, isolated monastery would afford Giles precious privacy from the curious, pitying glances of outsiders.

Father Stavroniketa made the sign of the cross and murmured, "*Kyrie eleison*—Lord, have mercy on this young man."

After the monk departed, Giles said, "Phillipa, come here."

She went to her lover. Standing close to him, she felt, as always, that sweet, sexual weakness, a sense of unbounded flowing into and through her, a flood of serenity and well-being that was the closest thing to mystical surrender people ever reached.

"You look rather like a rakish pirate," she teased, pressing her hips unashamedly against his, exulting in the hard thrust of his arousal. "Except you have two patches instead of one."

"You do know what pirates do to their captives, don't you?"

"Show me."

He aligned his hands with her jaw. Quickly, questioningly, he ran his fingers over her face, feeling its delicate contours, its sculptured angles and planes.

"My fingers tell me you are quite beautiful," he said in that low, seductive Welsh voice.

Yes, she thought in mild surprise, I will always be beautiful to him. Now I will never age. "You have deceiving fingers," she teased.

"My mind and my heart don't deceive me, Phillipa. I am very grateful for your love."

She didn't want his gratitude, she wanted his love. But this was a place to start. She felt her heart swell, and her embrace was as fierce as his.

Chapter 14

In the deep of night the rhythmic beat of the seman-tron, the mallet striking the wooden plank, awakened Phillipa. Father Stavroniketa had told her that Noah had summoned the animals into the ark with just such a resonant wooden plank and mallet. Now the seman-tron called the faithful into the spiritual ark, the monastery, for worship. It must be near dawn, she thought.

Careful not to disturb Giles, she propped herself on one elbow and turned on the lamp to study her be-loved's sleeping face. Some nights they didn't sleep but used the waning of darkness to explore each other's mind and body. They had both been delighted to real-ize that the exploration would never be complete, for their minds were infinite.

Even after a week at the monastery, that physical side of their love, that joining of their bodies, regardless of how often it was repeated, was insufficient for their needs. While they slept they pressed against each other, spoon fashion. If, during the night, they became parted, one of them would sleepily grope for the other until reassured.

The healed temple wound, partially concealed by Giles's rumpled hair, made a small fuchsia scar. With his thickly lashed lids closed in sleep, he was once again the perfect Greek god he had been the day she met him. Only his eyes themselves betrayed to the acute observer that something was amiss. Their once vividly intense blue color was now a paler, faded shade and appeared somewhat clouded by the otherwise undetectable scar tissue.

He began to thrash, and she knew he was having the recurring dream. He seemed to be coping with his wakening hours as a blind person, but, asleep, all his old fears of the coal mines and their terrible darkness surfaced. She touched his shoulder. "Giles," she said softly. "Giles, it's all right."

"How long have you been awake?" he asked, surprising her by cupping his hand behind her head.

"Not long. Are you hungry?"

"Ravenous." He pulled her face down to his, and his lips feasted on her kiss. Both of them were ravenous for life, finding that it tasted sweeter than ever.

He rolled atop her, and she laughed softly. "Do you know, my fine stallion, we must smell of our lovemaking. Whatever must the monks think when we eat with them?''

''I imagine they're close to renouncing their vows,'' he growled and began to rain kisses on her bare neck and shoulders.

That dawn—though for him there was no differentiating between night and daylight—they made love with an exquisitely full expression of their innate sexuality, a complete physical and psychological surrender, so that their capacity for pleasure was heightened to a level that she was certain few ever experienced. For her, it was a glorious revelation of love in all its degrees, shadings and complexities.

Afterward they dressed for breakfast at the rectory. As they donned their clothing they found excuses merely to touch one another, to be reassured of, if nothing else, their wondrous love.

Even as he stood naked before the bathroom's small sink, attempting to shave, she moved close beside him while she combed her hair so she could simply touch him, sway against him. It was as if they couldn't get enough of each other. She lived in dread of being permanently separated from him.

''You missed a patch—on your jaw,'' she said. ''Here, let me—''

''No,'' he said firmly. ''I'll find it.'' His hand rubbed his jaw, his fingers halting at the prickly spot.

He was so damned independent, she thought, watching him relather the small patch of stubble.

Though it was late July the dawn was chilly. Hand in hand, they walked along the stone path toward the rectory, where each morning they shared Spartan meals with the half dozen monks.

"Did you hear that rustle?" she asked.

"Yes. In the pine needles, wasn't it?"

"A brown-furred rabbit. I'm afraid we disturbed its sleep. It scampered off into a pile of dead leaves."

Giles's movements lacked the lithe gracefulness of the sighted. His stride had diminished to a cautious walk, but there was still that arrogant set of the shoulders, the proud tilt of the head, the carriage of a young man self-confident in his masculinity. "Has the sun risen yet?"

"Well, in the west the sky is still smattered with stars. But behind us it's awash with rosiness."

"You paint a beautiful word picture, Phillipa. You should have been a writer."

"I've sometimes thought about it. Doesn't everyone? You admitted the same once yourself."

After a mere seven days at the monastery she no longer had to tell him that the stone path curved just ahead.

"You know, Giles, I like it here. The sense of serenity and age-old ritual are comforting. Monks bowing, prostrating themselves, making rounds to kiss the icons, lighting and snuffing candles, that fervent chanting of theirs."

"It's a world apart, isn't it, love? I can understand how they can forget the demands of the outside world.

Here at the monastery I feel…I suppose you would call it life's secret rhythm."

"I know. I feel it, too."

"Father Stavroniketa was right about becoming renewed here. The monks' strenuous discipline revitalizes the body. It's something I'll have to acquire when I go back to the complexities of life."

"You've always been capable of strenuous discipline, Giles."

He grinned ruefully. "Not the kind that made me get up at four in the morning."

From the abbey came the sound of a cough, as the monks filed through a side door and took the smooth stone path toward the refectory. She half turned toward Giles, but kept her gaze on the path, always searching now for any new object—a pine cone, an overturned stone—that might present an obstacle for him. "You're coping much better than I ever could."

His smile was forced this time. "It's rather surprising to discover there's nothing to do but cope. Nothing. Absolutely nothing."

The refectory was a large white room with niches in the walls for icons, and a few dark-wood furnishings. The tables were covered in white cotton brocade and arranged in a U-shape. The monks, their sandaled feet shuffling on the brown-matted floor, filed in to stand before their places at the tables while the abbot blessed the food. Breakfast was a light meal, consisting of a kettle of coffee, a pot of warm milk and eggs and crusty rolls.

Since early morning was a time for reflection and meditation, only a few words were exchanged among the monks as they ate under the eyes of the painted saints lining the refectory walls. Surrounded by the monks and the solemn demeanor they wore at meal times she felt almost like a child, prone to giggling outbursts.

She felt positively youthful!

With a minimum of fuss she rearranged Giles's flatware so that the knife and spoon were on one side of the plate, the fork on the other. Quietly she told Giles what was on his plate and where, using the face of the clock method.

After they had eaten, a plump little monk named Brother Mynos brought the potent Flora, a herbal liqueur. Following a heavy meal, the drink was strong; when it followed a barely broken fast, she thought, it was staggering but wonderful.

"The best part of breakfast," Giles observed with a wry smile.

"Do you think we can smuggle some bottles to our guesthouse?" she teased.

"If not that, we can try bribery."

After breakfast the monks departed for their individual daytime tasks—in the kitchen, in the garden and at manual labor. She and Giles went for their daily midmorning stroll, although stroll was rather a mild term for the arduous climb among the sea-washed rocks.

"It's very dangerous," cautioned Father Stavroni-keta, the first time he had shown them the path. "To walk along it, eight-hundred feet over the Aegean, in a storm is an act of faith."

"To walk along it blind is a test of faith," Giles had quipped, but what he'd said was true. Without her guiding hand he couldn't have negotiated the obstacle course, despite the phenomenal memory he was beginning to demonstrate.

At the base of the cliff were various-size rocks, some as large as their guesthouse bathroom. There, below the gray cliffs, they had absolute privacy, and they would rest, stretching quite unashamedly nude in the lazy afternoon sun. She loved feeling its heat, loved the taste of the salt spray on Giles's skin.

The change in him was dramatic; all the coolness and reserve were gone now. Exposed to the raw power of nature—the sting of the salt-laden wind and the heat of the copper sun—they really talked.

The day was theirs until after Vespers, when the monastery gates would swing shut and everyone would turn in. She realized that she had never truly used her eyes before, and now that she had to see for both of them, she learned to make the fullest possible use of her sight.

"Out to sea, maybe midway between the coast and the horizon, there's a tanker of some sort. It's like a whale—long and bright silver where the sunlight reflects off it. Oh, Giles, on the rock below us—just off to your left—is a sea gull! All brown and white, with a small fish struggling in its bill.''

"I miss..." He didn't complete his thought, just stared sightlessly at the panorama of the sea.

She could imagine what he had been about to say. The yearning in his voice had been so poignant that she felt her heart squeeze painfully.

To fill in the silence she rattled off some history trivia. ''Do you know, Giles, that Darius lost his fleet out there in a vicious storm. Three hundred of the Persian king's ships and twenty thousand men were dashed on the rocks. In the fifth century, I think.''

"And just how do you come by so much knowledge?'' His voice was normal again. ''Father Stavroniketa?''

''Wrong. You mustn't forget, my dear boy, that you are talking to the wife of an archaeology professor.''

Instantly she regretted her words. She was no longer an older professor's wife, and Giles was no more a boy but so much a man.

Silence hovered over them again, broken only by the splash of the waves on the rocks. The blue-green water gave her an inspiration, and she said excitedly, ''Giles, do you like to swim?''

''After rugby, it's one of my favorite sports... or rather, it was.''

Yes, she thought, looking at the mass of muscles in his shoulders, his powerful physique was excellently suited to swimming. He had the build of an athlete, broad shoulders, and the tapering waist and hips that would offer no body drag against the water.

"I'll be right back," she said. "Don't move."

He grinned lazily. "I was thinking about taking a long hike."

"Don't you dare. Not without me." She tugged on jeans and a shirt. "It would be just like you to meet some comely mermaid, sunning herself on the rocks. I'll be back in less than fifteen minutes."

Nimbly she leaped from rock to slippery rock and made her way back up the slope to the monastery. On her way she passed one gray-bearded monk cutting old beams in a project to restore certain neglected areas of the monastery. Brother Paul and the other monks whom she saw several times a day, were beginning to seem almost like old friends.

Brother Paul happily directed her to Father Stavroniketa, who was her favorite. Within minutes Father Stavroniketa, leading her to a musty storage room, was able to satisfy her request. "We use the transistor radio during storm warnings," he told her, "but you two are more than welcome to borrow it while you are here."

Triumphantly she returned to Giles, who was reclining on the rocks, his body absorbing the life-renewing sunlight. At the sight of such masculine perfection she felt her lungs momentarily cease to function. She stifled the sensual excitement erupting inside her and picked her way over the rocks.

"That certainly didn't take you long," he said, turning sightless eyes toward her and offering a warm smile that wrenched her heart.

"Listen." She turned on the radio. A staccato Greek folksong was playing on the local station.

"A radio! A great idea."

"Better than you think."

"Oh?" he asked, perking up with interest at the innuendo in her voice.

She touched his shoulder, loving the feeling of his smooth, hot flesh under her fingers. "Giles, this way you can go swimming every day when the tide is out. With the volume turned high, the music will be a guide for you, so you'll know the direction of the shoreline."

She had expected excitement, but his serious response pleased her much more. He took her hand from his shoulder and turned her palm up to kiss it. "Phillipa," he whispered against her palm, "I love you. *Je t'aime*," and then in Italian, *"Te voglio bene."*

A midmorning swim became the pattern for the glorious summer days they spent at St. Nicolas. Despite what he had gone through, Giles's skin glowed with health, and his muscles were firm and hard and sleek.

After they swam they would eat lunch, often there on the rocks; then they would rest or stroll along the wooded paths within the monastery grounds. Sometimes they even walked through the fields that lay outside its walls.

"There are rows of vegetables and brilliantly colored flowers," she once told Giles, "as neat and orderly as an illustration from a medieval Book of Hours."

"Lavender," he said, his nostrils flaring to identify the flowers. "And lilac. Am I right?"

She laughed. "You forgot the sunflowers."

In the evening she would occasionally read to him from books borrowed from Father Stavroniketa. Some of them were surprisingly quite secular in nature.

"The monastery library is another matter—exactly what you would expect to find in the Middle Ages," she said, and described it to Giles. "Tons of dusty, but well-preserved manuscripts—fifteen thousand of them, Father Stavroniketa claims—most of them from the classical and medieval periods. But no one ever bothers to read them."

Sometimes Giles became impatient, and she intuitively knew that it wasn't the moment but the future that chafed him. One evening she was curled up in a corner of the sofa, trying to read a novel she had chanced to find. But more often than not her gaze strayed to linger on Giles, who seemed restless that night.

"Giles, why don't you seriously consider writing? Your exotic occupations—British Secret Service, liaison for an Arab potentate—would provide you with a wealth of material."

He set down the bottle of herbal liqueur she had persuaded one of the monks to part with. "I don't know, Phillipa. I'd have to give something like that a lot of thought. I'm quite certain that writing a novel isn't as easy as most people think. Besides, between my rusty typing and my blindness, the manuscript would be damned near indecipherable."

She watched him negotiate from between the sideboard and her chair with unerring accuracy. She knew by now not to offer more than minimal assistance or he would become quite irritated. The last thing she wanted was for him to resent his dependence on her. That would be a death knell for their love.

Teasingly she caught his hand and licked the sweetish liqueur drops from the tip of his forefinger, which he used as a gauge for ascertaining when a glass was full.

He chuckled, but she said, picking her words very, very cautiously as she went, "Giles, we've been living in each other's pocket for months now and I know you too well. You're worried, it's obvious, that to...to choose another occupation—"

His hand slipped out of hers and slid up her arm to grasp her hair, gently tilting her head back. He lowered his head and kissed her parted lips, then straightened. His expression was fierce. "Stop talking to me as if you were walking on eggshells. Speak your mind, Phillipa."

"All right. I think you're concerned that choosing an occupation that doesn't require the use of your eyes would be like admitting you're permanently blind. Am I right?"

Frowning, he slumped down in the deep cushioned sofa across from her. "I don't know," he said. "I don't know. Maybe you are. It's so bloody difficult to be objective about being blind."

Knowing that no words could comfort him, she rose and went to him, settling herself in his lap and laying her head on his shoulder. The heat of his sun-toasted flesh caressed her cheek. "It isn't a decision you have to make today or tomorrow, or even next year."

His hands unbuttoned her blouse and drew her breasts from her bra to lovingly caress them with his hands, then his mouth. His lips were hot as she pressed against him urgently. Quickly he shed his jeans, pushed her skirt above her waist and removed her panties.

His body meshed hungrily with hers, almost as if attempting to find sanctuary there. Her need for Giles's love was insatiable. Desperately her flesh sought union with his flesh. Within each other's encircling arms and legs they searched for and found refuge from the loneliness and the darkness.

As always in those precious days, they fused together completely and were made stronger by that fusion. Before St. Nicolas, before Giles had been blinded, their lovemaking had been both a mutual assuaging of the flesh and a spark struck from two minds meeting, but now it was something that transcended even that.

Afterward she collapsed on his chest, holding him close. And later, after the desperate demands of their bodies had been met, after they had drawn as close together as physical limitations would allow, the cou-

pling of their spirits began. They talked far into the
night, since they were no longer limited by the bound-
aries between daylight and darkness.

As time passed Giles's movements became more
confident, his stride longer, his sense of his body
stronger. At her side he learned to step out boldly,
knowing that she would guide or caution him with a
light touch or a word.

Relying on his memory, he moved easily around the
guesthouse, rarely bumping into anything, and she was
always cautious never to leave objects lying around—
shoes, books, throw pillows.

A week after her first conversation with Giles about
the possibility of his writing, she once again sought out
Father Stavroniketa.

"What can I help you with, my child?" the guestmaster asked, pushing back the sleeves that hung almost to the hem of his woolen robe. His forearms were
blanketed with dense hair and muscled from manual
labor.

"You don't have a typewriter here, do you, Father?"

His smile contrasted brightly against his black beard.
"Contrary to popular opinion, we no longer labori-
ously copy Biblical texts by hand. However, I fear our
typewriter is missing its capital R."

She smiled radiantly. "I won't tell Giles if you
don't."

He laughed. "How is he doing?"

A tiny line creased the bridge of her nose. "Here, at the monastery, fine. But you and I both know that the monastery is a world apart. What happens when we return to the demands of the old world..." She shrugged. "He's talked before of writing a novel. I thought that maybe with the use of the typewriter..." She shrugged again and offered a hopeful little smile.

For three days the typewriter set on the guest-house's dining room table, untouched. One afternoon, when they had returned from swimming and were both in a gay mood, she dared to ask, "When are you going to make a start on that book?"

Toweling his chest, he laughed and said, "Oh, in a couple of thousand of years, more or less."

"Let's make it less." She grinned, then laughed happily when he looped the damp towel to encircle her shoulders. She could easily have dodged, but she wanted very, very much to be caught.

"Tomorrow I'll start. I promise." Drawing her closer with the towel, he dipped his head, murmuring, "I'll seal the promise with a kiss."

That night the sematron awakened her again. As before, she turned on the nightlight with a modicum of motion, so as not to disturb Giles. She planned to pick up the half-read novel on the nightstand, but for a moment her attention was caught by her beloved's handsome face, his thick dark brown lashes that were counterpoint to his golden skin.

Never had she felt so vital and eager, so blooming with love. Love, she thought, made one ageless. She knew she made Giles happy, and because she did, her own happiness was complete. She was boundlessly grateful for what she had with Giles—something very wonderful. Strong and bright and wonderful. And she knew she would protect that happiness with her life.

Brushing his eyes with a sleep drowsy hand, Giles rolled away from her. She knew she hadn't moved and disturbed him. Uneasily she pushed the unsettling thought from her mind.

The next day, as they picked their way down to their private cove, she watched Giles's lithe movements over the slippery rocks. She noticed that he occasionally turned his head momentarily away from the strong sunlight. She doubted that he was even aware of what he was doing.

But *she* was. Apparently he had some light perception, which meant that the doctor had been wrong, that somehow light was registering on healthy retinas.

Somewhere in her brain a little voice whispered, Surely Phillipa, you know the difference between holding a hand and chaining a soul.

Chapter 15

It started out with trifling arguments. Their weeks of idyllic isolation had been broken by only an occasional visit with Father Stavroniketa and meals with the other four monks. The solitude was taking its toll on both Phillipa and Giles.

A confrontation had been bound to occur sooner or later. Both of them secretly realized that their relationship was built on an illusion, a fantasy. How that relationship would sustain itself in the face of hard reality was a matter still to be tested.

Giles stepped out of the shower, reaching unerringly for the fluffy towel on the rack. He felt great. Yesterday he had started on his novel. For some time now, ever since Phillipa had proposed the idea of writing a novel, he had been thinking about it in the back of his mind.

Initially he had toyed with plots for a suspense novel, as she had suggested. He had planned to set it in Afghanistan, using an English adventurer, collaborating with a young Greek woman, as the focal character. Phillipa . . . wise, serene, lovely Phillipa . . . was to have been the model for his heroine.

But over the ensuing days a different idea had germinated and taken root—a story based on his years in the coal mines. Not a story about himself, because he knew he was too close to that part of his past to be objective.

What if, he silently argued as he wrapped the towel around his waist, what if he took a boy from the age of seven, when he entered the mines, and showed his blighted existence, showed his thwarted attempts over the years to improve his lot, to escape the hopeless life preordained for him?

And then what if . . .

With the bathroom door closed and the room thick with steam, the scent of Phillipa's perfume was intensified. It pervaded the guesthouse, even when she wasn't there. The scent of honeysuckle and lilac filled his nostrils and expanded in his head so that he was full of her, wanting her all over again, even though they had made love only hours earlier. Last night they had taken their pleasure in each other in one of a dovecote of musty cells abandoned by medieval hermits.

Amazing, he thought, the places he and Phillipa found when the urge to make love overpowered discretion: the cool recesses of a grotto; the ruins of a former shepherd's hut; even within the concealment of high sweet summer grass laden with lavender. Bees from the monks' apiary nearby had put a short but laughter-filled end to that tryst.

He simply couldn't get enough of her, this Lady Phillipa who was such an aristocrat in public and such a marvelous wanton in private. At times he was awed by her capabilities. The combination of her incisive intelligence with her infinite patience and determination made her a formidable foe and an intriguing woman.

Opening one of the cabinets high above the sink, he reached for his shaving foam. The can wasn't in its usual place. Or else he wasn't. He paused, getting his bearings. His hands assured him that he was directly in front of the sink. The cabinet he wanted had to be the first one to the right.

He tried again, his hands groping futilely for the squat can—or even, as confirmation of the right location, his razor or after-shave lotion. Could he have stored the items in the wrong cabinet?

He began a systematic search of the other cabinets. One, he knew, contained towels and washcloths. The next, bars of soap and shampoo and other toilet articles. When he knocked a can onto the counter he cursed liberally in Welsh under his breath.

Phillipa must have heard the loud clatter all the way downstairs, because she called out, "Giles? Are you all right?"

"Of course I'm all right!"

His fingers slid along the counter until they encountered a can, a tall one. Not his shaving foam but Phillipa's hair spray. "Damn!"

"Giles, whatever is it?" she asked from the bathroom doorway.

Taken by surprise, he spun around, knocking the hair spray can onto the floor, where it rolled against his instep. "You know better than to sneak up on me like that!"

"I wasn't sneaking." Her tone was pleasant and full of patience.

He tried to keep the annoyance out of his voice. "I can't find my shaving things."

"That's because I forgot to tell you I moved them to within easy reach. There, at the back of the counter— on your left. I was worried that you might cut yourself on the razor, groping above your head for it."

The way she talked, as if communicating with a slow-witted child, infuriated him. "If you would stop to think," he said, his words clipped and spaced, "you would realize that, unlike those who can see, I am always groping, whether what I want is above my head or at counter level. The next time you arbitrarily decide to move something, I would appreciate it if you would inform me about the move—especially when the items you have moved happen to belong to me."

"There won't be a next time!" she snapped. "As far as I'm concerned, you can damned well put away your own personal effects from now on!"

He listened to her footsteps taking her away from him. A gut-wrenching feeling hit him. What was he doing, driving her away from him like this? He started after her and heard the downstairs door slam shut. By the time he could pull on a pair of jeans, she'd be gone.

He turned back toward the bathroom. Perhaps it would be better if each of them was alone for a while, with time to cool off and sort out their thoughts.

He changed directions and headed for the balcony. Phillipa once said it was like daring fate to stand out on the rickety platform. He rather liked the unseen challenge—feeling the wind tug at his hair and sting his eyes, and hearing the sea crash on the rocks directly below.

The powerful elements reaffirmed his sense of his being part of the scheme of life. In fact, the monastery itself offered a better perspective, an improved sense of proportion, a fund of serenity that he sensed he would need to draw on later. Focusing on the eternal—whether the waves or God—had a way of cutting the overwhelming, apparently insuperable present down to size.

There was a time when he would never have questioned his inner strengths. After surmounting all the difficulties and obstacles of his childhood, he had become a man who was completely and utterly sure of his capabilities. Others might falter, but he would never fail himself.

Surprising, how a physical impairment could affect his vital life forces. He had been so arrogantly certain of the strength and power of his mind and spirit, so sure he could rely on them.

Now, fight it though he did, he was beginning to resent his dependence on Phillipa. It wasn't her fault. His resentment wasn't fair to her—or to their love.

At first he had been grateful for her devotion, and it had seemed to him that they had forged a bond of something even greater than love, a bond that seemed inviolable. Now he no longer felt like the strong and capable man he had been, and this insidious feeling was seeping into their love life, which they had both thought could never be diminished.

His hands gripped the wooden rail so tightly that splinters dug into his palms. He couldn't let that precious bond be destroyed. Somehow he would have to dig down deep within his psyche and find some inner resource to combat this outer weakness.

Humility.

For him, humility had always been a sign of weakness. As far as he was concerned, the meek didn't inherit the earth—they worked the earth for the strong of will.

From downstairs came the sounds of the front door opening and closing. The sound of Phillipa's light step across the floor told him that she had returned. He expelled a sigh that was almost a groan. He was going to have to go against all his values and tenets, but just maybe...if he could learn to lay aside his ego.

That evening they both tried to pretend nothing had happened. Their little guesthouse, though, was closing in on them. If Phillipa had turned a page of the novel she was reading in the past ten minutes, he hadn't heard it. He could feel her eyes on his back.

His own novel held little interest for him. The first page contained only the one paragraph he had typed, and that had been so long ago that he couldn't remember the exact words. He could ask Phillipa to read them back, but to do so would only reinforce his helplessness.

What he needed was renewed interest in the book, but his mind was on Phillipa. Such a lovely, incandescent lady, such a scintillating woman. Even sightless, he could still see with his mind's eye the ivory sheen of her flawless skin, the slightly darker, rich honey color of her nipples, could remember how, at the touch of his fingertips, they grew full and hard.

Phillipa...Phillipa...Phillipa. Her name was a pulsing rhythm in his brain.

Why not admit it? He was aching with the want and need of her.

"How about a walk?" she asked with a brightness he doubted she felt.

"Why not." He yanked the sheet of paper out of the typewriter and wadded it, tossing it onto the table.

"Why did you do that, Giles?"

He heard the puzzlement mixed with reproach in her voice and felt instant contrition. "I wasn't that pleased with what I had written. I can't even remember what the hell I said. Shall we go?"

Since arriving at the monastery he had reverted to the ways of childhood, going barefoot and shirtless except for mealtimes in the refectory. He did so now, silently counting the number of steps from the guesthouse stoop to the main path. At his side Phillipa said nothing, merely touching his elbow if he veered off the path, which he rarely did these days.

Because the monastery's gates were already closed she suggested a stroll along one of the graveled *allées* by the chapel, a converted seventeenth-century stable. Once they passed the earthy smell of the stable, wild thyme, boxwood and pine needles scented the air. The sway of cypresses in the wind reached his ever-alert ears, as did the raucous twittering of magpies and the musical call of other birds he wasn't familiar with. He figured dusk must be near.

"Giles..."

"Yes?" He winced as his toe hit a sharp stone on the path.

"I've been thinking. How would you feel about using a tape recorder to write your novel?" She hurried on, her forced lightness annoying him, because he knew she was trying to conceal her anxiety.

"That way you wouldn't have to worry about remembering, or depending on me to read back what—I know how that irritates you. When you finish a first draft we can have the cassettes transcribed. Then—''

''Phillipa, why don't you let me run my life my own way? I don't try to run yours.''

He didn't have to see her to know that her body had stiffened. The crunch of her espadrilles on the gravel had subtly changed.

Pain and frustration sharpened her voice. ''You know, Giles, I think Damon picked the perfect place for us! A retreat for hermits. That's what you should become. A hermit! You'd be much happier that way than trying to cope with your blindness in the real world.''

His hand found her shoulder, and he spun her around to face him. ''Now you listen to me! I'm—''

He broke off, realizing that his fingers were digging into her soft shoulders, that he was shaking her. At once he released her and turned away.

''Giles?''

He ignored the plea in her voice. Didn't she understand that the love they had left would begin to dissipate, that in a week, a month, a year, it would all be gone? He couldn't stand to watch the corrosive cancer of his anxiety and resentment destroy their once beautiful and invulnerable relationship.

Thrusting his hands in his jeans pockets, he walked away, halting only when she lightly touched his elbow. ''The path skirts a tree just ahead, remember?''

Without turning back to her, he said, his voice as cold as the waters of a fjord, ''You're right. About the hermit stuff. I just don't want to make the compromises necessary for the kind of life you would want to lead. Look, Phillipa, I can't deny that sex between us has been terrific, but I'm much too accustomed to doing things my own way. Even more so now.

"Besides..." He paused, carefully choosing his words. "Since the bombing I've come to realize how important each moment is. There are things I've always wanted to do and never had the time. Now is the time, while I'm still in the prime of my life. You've already lived a full life. You've done your living and loving."

"You arrogant bastard," she breathed.

He knew that she was devastated by his cold-blooded remarks, her sense of femininity sliced to the quick. He waited to hear her march away, but she surprised him. She grabbed his forearm and turned him around to face her.

"You haven't got the foggiest notion what living and loving are all about, Giles Hayes-David. But I'm going to teach you, and you will bloody well learn!"

With that she wrapped her arms around his neck and kissed him full on the lips. That sweet mouth moved over his tenderly, lovingly, and he wanted to weep for his cruelty. Then she stepped away from him, and he could feel the heat of her anger. "There. Since you're so accustomed to doing things your own way, you can find your own way back to the guesthouse!"

He stood where he was, listening to her stalk off until the crunch of gravel could no longer be heard. She was all lady, he thought, and all tigress.

Finding his way back wasn't that difficult. He had walked the path enough to know its direction. Every so often, when the gravel beneath his feet thinned out, he knew he was veering off the trail.

Still, Phillipa startled him when, not five minutes later, she said, "Dammit all, Giles, you're going to run into that sycamore again."

He couldn't help but grin. "Is it safe to make love right here on the path, or is someone watching?"

"The gravel will bruise my bottom. Let's go home, you randy old goat."

Chapter 16

Across from Phillipa and Giles, Father Stavroniketa drank the coffee she had prepared and talked of the monastery. "Karpeta has been a religious community since 1034, two hundred years before the monastery was built. But all sorts of people seek retreat here. Some years ago a French president who was defeated for reelection brought his defeat and his dignity here to St. Nicolas."

"To reflect on the value of *la gloire* in the light of eternity?" Giles asked with a dry smile and took a sip of the coffee.

"Exactly, my son." The monk's smile flashed. Phillipa really enjoyed his occasional visits. "We do for the spirit what a spa does for the body."

Privately, very privately, Phillipa was thinking of what Giles did for *her* body. Father Stavroniketa's unannounced visit had interrupted a most passionate entanglement of arms and legs. Her satisfaction had been postponed, and there she sat so serenely, hot with her own wanting.

Over her cup she glanced at Giles. Blindness didn't blunt the vitality that radiated from him. His features had the hard edges of youth. She swallowed her coffee, but a lump was still lodged in her throat, a lump of secret agony. The argument she had had with Giles two days before had been only one of an increasing number, small disagreements for the most part.

Rationally she understood why he had said the ugly, spiteful things he had. She understood that he was afraid his resentment at being blind would eventually wound her, would leave a scar that time wouldn't heal. He had wanted to spare her that.

But she knew better. She was much stronger than he realized. She was strong enough for both of them.

What worried her was the certainty that his concern with their age differences was always in the back of his mind, whether he recognized the fact or not. Those fourteen years might not make that much difference to him now, but later they would.

The gap in their ages wasn't the only worry that was pulling her apart inside. As she and Giles bade Father Stavroniketa goodbye a half hour later, she still hadn't resolved the conflict inside her.

In fact, the decision-making process took another two days, but she finally brought herself to accept her conclusion. Implementing her decision would be the most difficult thing she would ever have to do.

When at last she did, she knew that Giles sensed her lie and was hurt by it. "I need to go away for a day, to shop in Karpeta." She bent over and kissed his temple, where the scar was. "You know how women are, Giles. We need to get back to the frivolous pleasures of the world every so often."

His fingers, such strong fingers, stilled on the keyboard. "You're right, of course," he said in a negligent tone, as if to impress upon her his unconcern. "Have a good time."

He had already typed thirty-two pages of his book, which he had entitled *Out of the Darkness*. She had read each page back to him as he finished it, offering her suggestions if he asked for them. She had been unstinting with her criticism as with her praise. Some of her suggestions he accepted, others he didn't.

Regardless, the hours they had shared working on the story had bonded them in yet another way.

That was why this trip was so agonizing. In the rented Volvo she drove out of the monastery gates with a sense of foreboding that left her feeling almost physically ill. She made the trip to Constantine in just over two hours. Although she didn't have an appointment, she was admitted within fifteen minutes to the office of the doctor who had operated on Giles.

She sat across the immense desk from the dry, humorless doctor and related her suspicion in terse unemotional words. "Because I've noticed Giles unconsciously reacting to bright lights, I thought I had better let you know, although I doubt it's anything."

Dr. Nicolaidis toyed with his ball-point pen for a moment, then said, "I could very well have been wrong about the prognosis at the time of the operation. It would seem, from what you have told me, Lady Phillipa, that the retinas may not have been damaged, after all. If this is true, we could try a corneal transplant. You will need to convince Mr. Hayes-David to come in for a test first."

She swallowed painfully. "I don't think that would be any problem, doctor."

Dr. Nicolaidis leaned forward and said in a sterner note, "It could very well turn out to be a problem. He must understand what he faces. If he gets his hopes up and then is severely disappointed, the mental stress could be overwhelming, possibly more than he could cope with. You must prepare him to face the possibility that the tests or the operation could have negative results. Even the strongest of people can break under those conditions."

She rose and extended her hand. "I understand. Thank you, doctor."

His feminine-agile fingers clasped hers. "I must remind you, Lady Phillipa, that his retinas had, at the very least, been torn. Any jarring, such as a nasty bump on the head, could cause the retinas to detach this time, and Mr. Hayes-David would then be, as we thought at first, blind for life." To ease the grimness of his statement he smiled and added, "I'd advise him to forgo his rugby and other such sports until we make the tests."

"I think we can safely exclude rugby, along with roller derby."

The doctor's sparse brows shot up over the rim of his glasses. "Roller derby?"

"Nothing, nothing. Thank you so much, Dr. Nicolaidis. I'll be back in touch with you."

She made several more stops in Constantine, one at a boutique to purchase a blue silk Valentino head scarf as evidence of a day supposedly spent shopping. Then she began the two-hour return drive to the monastery. During this time she waged another bitter battle within herself.

Giles was happy with her.

But he would be happier with his sight.

Giles, beautiful and vital and brilliant. With sight, he would eventually have to acknowledge her for what she was: simply an older woman with whom he had become temporarily infatuated because of her age and experience.

What it came down to, she told herself with painful honesty, was the bald fact that if he recovered his eyesight, she would probably lose him, if not immediately, then sometime in the future, when she had become haggard and he was still, as he had prophesied, in his prime.

During the drive back she came face-to-face with the realization that she was not as emotionally strong as she had once so proudly thought herself. Issues of ethics and principle wavered in her mind. What she saw was an ugly portrait of her innermost person, what the French called her *esprit*.

She made it back to the monastery just before the gates closed for the night. Her footsteps carried her feverishly back to the little guesthouse. His torso bare above his jeans, Giles was sitting on the worn stone sill, his head tilted back against the wooden door. The last rays of a dying sun played across his skin, and she stopped twenty yards down the path and, for a brief moment, lovingly caressed him with her eyes.

"Phillipa?" His head was canted, listening. His eyes, wide open, intelligent and expressive, seemed to look slightly to one side of her, and she had a powerful impulse to turn and glance behind her, following their steady gaze. She hadn't moved, but his senses had developed to such an acute level that he somehow knew she was standing there.

"How did you know I was here?" she asked, coming forward to kneel before him.

He grinned. "The air carried your scent. You found something to buy?"

He would know she had. He must have heard the rustle of the bags she carried. "I most certainly did. A blue head scarf for me. And for you—a tape recorder. It was the only one in Karpeta." She was amazed at how easily she was learning to lie these days. "And I'm giving it to you only with the provision that I get ten percent of the royalties from *Out of the Darkness*."

He laughed. "Done. Now come here."

She set her things down on the path and moved closer to him, taking his handsome face between her hands. "I missed you too much to enjoy shopping. Oh, God, but I love you so, Giles Hayes-David."

He caught her hands and rose, pulling her against his steely length. "Without your voice and touch to break the day, I grew bored. Writing became a chore, and I found the slightest excuses to get up from the typewriter and prowl the house. I missed you, too, love!"

"You just missed me reading your magnum opus back to you."

"Hush." His lips groped blindly but joyously for hers. Then he drew her inside the guesthouse that had become their love nest, and she forcibly put from her mind the news she had to tell him.

Later, as they lay entwined, half-asleep, her news burned inside her brain, yet she couldn't bring herself to say anything. She wasn't ready yet to share him with anybody else.

Not yet. Not just yet. A few more days.

The next afternoon she sat on the rocks and watched Giles's arms cutting steadily through the gentle waves, the water whipped to froth by the chopping of his powerful legs. At her side the transistor radio loudly played a romantic tune that did not put her in a romantic mood. She hadn't slept at all the night before. Her eyes felt sandy, and her head ached with fatigue.

She didn't have to tell Giles immediately, did she? Given time, one part of her mind insisted, his love for her would grow so that nothing else mattered.

When he scaled the rocks and came to her, grinning, she turned down the radio and handed him a towel. She was amazed at the confidence with which he negotiated the slippery, treacherous boulders. What if he should fall, hitting his head?

She knew then that she would have to tell him. His sight was going to be a costly gift for her to give him, but it would be worth it.

"Giles, we . . . I must tell you some—"

"It's going to storm," he said, his thick dark brows meeting over the bridge of his nose in a frown. "I can smell it in the air and feel it in the shift of the wind."

She glanced at the horizon. He was right. Angry clouds boiled above the sea line. At that very moment a harsh warm wind came in off the seas, ruffling the water and churning it into white waves that slapped petulantly against the rocks. The fishing boats along the curve of the far shore tugged restlessly at their mooring ropes.

She looked back to Giles, studying his eyes, as she so often did now. Their calm, level gaze possessed a mystical depth and a stoic acceptance of his affliction that she found awesome.

She couldn't do it; she couldn't tell him, not yet. Tonight. Tonight she'd tell him, after they had made love for what might be the last time.

"You had something to tell me?" he asked, draping the damp towel around his neck.

Even though he couldn't see her, she was unable to meet his steady gaze. Her cowardice was unconscionable. Averting her face, she said lightly, "Yes, I'm hungry for lunch. And you?"

"I'm hungry for you."

"Well, my love, you took so long bedding me the first time, I hope you've mastered the technique."

His delighted laughter was deep, full-bodied. "You've become quite risqué. I seem to be a bad influence on you. Let's go back up to the house, and I'll do my best after a reinforcing lunch to demonstrate my progress in the area of lovemaking."

In the kitchen he worked deftly alongside her, helping prepare a light tuna salad. He was near enough for her to sway against him and feel his reassuring masculine presence. It was as though, she thought forlornly, she were the blind one and not he.

"Something's bothering you," he said quietly as he diced celery. "What is it?"

She should have known he would pick up on her mood. He was so damned perceptive. She braced her hands on the counter, head bowed, and confessed in a dry, neutral voice, "I didn't just go shopping in Karpeta yesterday, Giles. I went to see Dr. Nicolaidis."

His knife went still. Puzzlement etched his voice. "Why?"

"Because I've suspected for several days now that you may not be permanently blind…the way you turn your head toward light and shadows. Dr. Nicolaidis agreed with me about the possibility. Tests will need to be run, of course. But he felt that, in spite of your torn retinas, there's a very good possibility of restoring your vision with corneal transplants. When I saw you scrambling over the rocks today, I knew I had been wrong to withhold the news from you, since a fall could destroy your chances."

"Why didn't you tell me at once?"

She heard the undercurrent of frustration mixed with hurt in his tone. Drawing a steadying breath, she answered in a low, almost inaudible voice, "Because these precious moments...the feelings we share...will never be the same, Giles. I admit it was selfish of—"

"You had so little faith in our love?" He slammed down the knife and turned away from her. "Please, Phillipa," he said wearily. "I want to be alone for a while. I need to think."

She looked at the forbidding breadth of his shoulders and knew that she deserved his contempt. An inaudible sigh drifted past her lips. "I understand." Listlessly she walked into the living room, picked up her head scarf and left the guesthouse.

For several long, agonizing minutes Giles stood rigid, until the surge of anger ebbed and calm reason took its place. He could understand Phillipa's reluctance to tell him, to instigate such an immense change in their relationship. She undoubtedly felt that its depth was founded on his affliction. Hadn't he once feared she would take another lover, a more mature, older man, her equal in ways he wasn't?

But his attempt at rational thinking was thwarted by the spark of hope her news had generated. Oh, God, to be able to see again! Precious sight!

A howling wind rattled the windows, and he realized she would be caught in the coming downpour. Abruptly he swerved away from the counter and rushed from the guesthouse. Outside the wind had picked up and the trees were thrashing in its force. He stood on the porch, tense, trying to judge where she would have gone. The summer storm coming in off the sea would have ruled out the treacherous path trailing down to their cove. Possibly she had gone to talk with Father Stavroniketa, or had taken a walk along one of the trails that meandered through the forest.

He had opened his mouth to call out for her when another voice reached his ears first. "The woman wearing the blue head scarf—over there beneath the trees!"

"I can't tell if that's her or not."

Giles's blood congealed. He recognized the last voice: the Oracle of Delphi! Never, in all the weeks since he had lost his sight, had he felt more helpless. In a flash he realized there was one way he could help her: at the possible expense of his eyesight. Perhaps even his life. All his instincts for self-preservation rejected the magnitude of such a sacrifice. It was so much to ask of a human being . . . and yet . . .

There wasn't even time to think further. He dashed from the shelter of the porch, trusting only his memory of the cliff path. "Come on, you bastards!" he shouted, hoping against hope that he could at least lead them away from Phillipa.

Behind him voices yelled, "That's him! That's the guy who was with her that night."

"Get him!" The voice of the Oracle.

Small, wind-tossed branches thrashed Giles's face and shoulders, and he corrected his course back onto the narrow path. It was impossible for him to count his steps. Yet he knew at once when the path merged with the cliff. The roar of the surf below him was louder, the wind stronger, buffeting him with its strength. The face of the sea would be furrowed in anger.

He started down the steep, rocky trail. He figured his odds were more equal here. Not only was he more familiar with the way, but surely, with such a storm coming in off the sea, the sky would be dark, making it difficult for the MPA men to see. He pushed away the terrifying thought that a mere slip, a slight knock on his head...

Below, he could hear waves slamming over the boulders, walls of water battering walls of rock. He recalled Father Stavroniketa's words, "I always fear this next stretch. It's along a cliff, with a straight drop to the sea. To walk along the path is an act of faith."

Suddenly he slipped. Flailing, he latched on to a scraggly pine sapling that left splinters in his palms. Quickly he scrambled to his feet and slid down the trail.

A loud, piercing scream that diminished in volume until it was swallowed by the sound of wind and waves told Giles that one of his pursuers had tempted fate and lost. How many more were left?

The storm howled unabated. As he neared the bottom of the cliff, the winds grew worse. Blindly he forged ahead, bone weary, wet to the skin. Finally he reached the base of the cliff. Behind him, very near, he heard a shout of rage.

How far to jump to the next slippery rock? Breakers roared too close. A hot sweat mingled with the icy cold saltwater on his face. This time Phillipa wasn't here to advise him.

A hand clutched his shoulder. "You're finished, Hayes-David!"

The Oracle!

Giles drove a fist toward his unseen opponent. He felt the man stagger with the impact. Then a mighty punch caught Giles on the collarbone. It snapped in two as easily as a twig. Pain shot through him. The next swing would find a truer target, he knew: his head. Instinctively he ducked, hoping to protect his head.

Unseeing, he dived for where he thought his opponent's midsection would be. A loud grunt exploded from the man as Giles's shoulder slammed him down onto a broad stone ledge. Wrenching pain shot from Giles's broken collarbone through his body, but he came up fighting, anyway. Waves poured over the two while they grappled and rolled, struggling for supremacy.

Giles, his hearing acute from having to compensate for his lack of sight, heard it first: the sound of a tremendous breaker roaring toward the rocks. He released his grip on the man and blindly, frantically, grabbed for any kind of handhold. His finger clawed at a small rocky protuberance. The man latched on to Giles's leg with a death clutch. The lethal wave hit, and Giles's fingernails tore with his effort to cling to the rock.

His opponent was not as fortunate. His death grip on Giles's leg loosened, slipped—and then Giles heard his panicky scream, which was lost in the crash of the wave. Seconds later the wave receded, taking Giles's nemesis with it back into the sea.

Chapter 17

Warm summer sunlight streamed into the hospital room, making a halo of the turban of white bandages that swathed Giles's head. A halter of some kind of elastic material held his collarbone in place. Stiff and uncomfortable, he sat in the chair opposite the bed, impatiently awaiting Dr. Nicolaidis's morning visit.

After he'd spent eight interminable days recuperating, the moment had at last arrived for the removal of the bandages. They were about to find out whether the corneal transplant had been a success.

Not only was Dr. Nicolaidis late, but so was Phillipa. And by more than thirty-five minutes. For the past ten days she had been arriving promptly at eight, when breakfast was served. Sometimes she read to him, sometimes they talked, and sometimes it had been enough just to sit with her in silence. Her abiding love had made the agony of waiting easier. He detested the antiseptic smell of the hospital and of himself, and couldn't wait until he was discharged.

"Who's there?" he asked, sensing another presence in the room. "Dr. Nicolaidis?"

"How did you know anyone was here?"

"Father Murphy." He smiled. "I felt the movement of air. And then smelled you."

"I smell that bad?"

"Wine and garlic."

"Let's see, I was blessing wine and—"

Giles chuckled. "Don't bother to explain, Father. I wouldn't want your explanation to besmirch your heavenly record."

"Well, well, the important day has finally arrived, hasn't it?"

"At last." Gingerly he shifted in the chair. "Where's Phillipa?"

"I have news that will certainly interest you, my son. Two bodies washed ashore this week five miles from the St. Nicolas Monastery. They belonged to Yeorgi Kannost and—" he paused to add import to his words "—Major Veranos."

"Veranos? Veranos was the Oracle?"

"His fingerprints on a Renault found parked just outside the monastery gates provided confirmation. The PFF believes Veranos was able to pull off all that he did—giving away state secrets, the bombings—due to the simple fact that as commander of internal security, he was privy to everything that went on."

"That's why the café was bombed," Giles mused, gradually assimilating the new information. "Veranos thought that Damon was in the limo that had gone to the café, didn't he?"

"Yes, Damon was the target, you see. And no one ever suspected Veranos."

"But we suspected you, Father. At least for a time."

"Don't you think I was aware of that? But the arrest of a third party working with Veranos—"

"A short, stocky man?"

"Yes. His name is Dimitri Yannis. He confessed to everything. Veranos had sold out to the Macedonian Provisional Army for a large sum of money and promises of power."

"Well, I'll be damned."

"I surely hope not, my son," the priest said, and both chuckled at the old joke between them. Then he added, "Apparently Veranos and Kannost followed Phillipa when she left the doctor's office."

At the mention of Phillipa, Giles repeated his question. "Where is she?"

Father Murphy's silence was thundering in Giles's ears. He leaned forward, hands clutching the arms of his chair hard enough to make him wince at the pain in his still-healing nails. "Where is she?" he demanded.

"She left, Giles."

"Where?" He tried to rise from the chair, and immediately Father Murphy was there, placing a gentle but restraining hand on his shoulder.

"Truly, I don't know. She asked me not to let you know just yet that she was leaving, but she never said where she was going. She has great faith that your sight will be restored, and she told me it was in your best interest that she left you now."

Giles had always known that somewhere in the world was the one woman meant for him. And now... "I'll find her, Father," he said. "I'll find her if it takes the rest of my life!"

The old aristocratic families of Britain had always been rooted in the countryside, vast tracts of which they had once ruled like fiefdoms. Under a clear sapphire sky Rothingham looked just as Giles had imagined, at least, if he discounted the slight cloudiness that etched his peripheral vision—a condition Dr. Nicolaidis had said would correct itself within a couple of months.

Rothingham was nestled in the depths of rural Berkshire on twelve hundred emerald acres. Despite its impressive size, the three-story house possessed a cozy warmth and charm that had evolved over the centuries. Gray-green ivy laced its stone pilasters and red-brick quoining.

Strange, Giles thought, as he lifted the heavy brass door knocker, how he noticed the varying shades of colors now. They seemed more brilliant than they ever had before he'd lost his sight.

A maid in a black poplin uniform admitted him to the great hall, with its vaulted ceiling, and a brief glance around the room nearly took his breath away. Aladdin's cave was the first thought that came to his mind—magnificent paneling, Beauvais tapestries, eighteenth-century antiques, marquetry furniture and masterworks by Van Dyck, Reynolds and Gainsborough.

"The master will be with you in a moment," the potato-plump woman told him, then left him to peruse the treasures, roped off with velvet cord for the daily tours. Small brass plaques identified the works, their dates and whether they belonged to the family or were on loan from various landed gentry.

A lanky but nice-looking silver-haired man in tweeds strolled briskly into the hall and offered his hand. "Giles Hayes-David? Of course you are. Phillipa has described you perfectly."

Giles's pulse quickened with excitement. Then she was here! He had been positive that this was where she would have gone. "And you are Sir Guy—"

"Please, just Guy. Congratulations on the success of your operation. Come into the drawing room. We can have tea there."

"Phillipa told you about my blindness?"

"Yes, but I would have guessed something was about, anyway. She was acting as impatient as an expectant mother the day your bandages were removed. She called Dr. Nicolaidis several times that day."

At that bit of news Giles's spirits soared. He glanced around the drawing room and recognized some of the works of art—an ancient Harewood Aphrodite attributed to Praxiteles—among a gallery of family portraits. "Museums would impoverish themselves for what you have here."

"We impoverish ourselves just trying to keep up the place. This spring we discovered the Georgian wing had dry rot, and last year the orangery came crashing down and had to be cleared out. Moreover, the entire roof recently had to be releaded."

"Then you must do quite a tourist business to keep the place up."

"Visitors account for only ten percent of what we need. Some funds come from the farms and various activities on the grounds, like the antique shop. I hope that Rothingham will continue to be inherited by people as dedicated to it as Robert and Phillipa and I are."

"Phillipa...how is she?"

Her older brother frowned, his white mustache curling downward with the ends of his mouth. "Well, I would say she seemed fine, maybe a little fatigued, the last time we talked."

Giles's heart plummeted to the pit of his stomach. "The last time?"

"Why, yes. Here's the tea, Giles. Do you take milk or sugar?"

"Neither." Anxiously he waited until the maid departed, then asked, "Phillipa's not here now?"

Guy looked uncomfortable. He lifted his hand-painted teacup to take a sip, then set it down in a saucer decorated with pale pink roses. "No, she left after spending only three weeks here."

Giles seethed. He had been confined to his hospital bed for two weeks—precious days wasted, when he could have been looking for Phillipa. He leaned forward and said in a voice taut with urgency, "Guy, I love your sister. Please, do you know where she went?"

"Look, it's none of my business, really. Phillipa never directly indicated her feelings for you. She merely described you as a dear young man with whom she had worked on an undercover operation in Macedonia."

Giles's mouth twisted. "She has this harebrained idea that I'm too young for her. As if age has anything to do with love. Her pride is all that's standing between us and our happiness."

"Ahh, yes, I could tell you a lot about our family's stubborn pride. Virtual war stories. I will tell you that I think Phillipa cares much more for you than she let on to me. But, honestly, I don't have the foggiest idea where she might have gone when she left here. She's always been the independent one. While Robert and I stayed on here, nurtured in the bosom of family and friends, she was always off on an adventure of one kind or another. I think marrying that archaeologist, Fleming, was an adventure for her. Working undercover for the PFF was another."

Giles's shoulders slumped. "She could be anywhere in the world." Wearily he set down his teacup and stood. "I appreciate all you've told me. When you next hear from Phillipa, will you tell her that I love her more than anything in this or any other world?" He should have been embarrassed to utter such a passionate declaration of love. The old Giles would have been. "Tell her, please, that I'm waiting for her at Cambria."

"Cambria?"

"My estate in Wales."

"I'll tell her, but as I said, old chap, my sister is quite proud. I doubt your message will change her mind."

With a grunt of exasperation Giles ripped the blank sheet of paper out of the typewriter. He had thought writing a second novel would be a snap after wading through the first. A rather foolish deduction, especially when he had yet to sell *Out of the Darkness*.

On the advice of his American agent he had even incorporated the ordeal of his blindness into the novel. That had been the most difficult part to write, because he was still too close to that harrowing time...and each page had reminded him of Phillipa.

Not that he needed to be reminded of her. Three months might have passed since his operation, but her lovely, heart-shaped face and warm, caramel-colored eyes were still as fresh in his mind as the day he had last seen them...the day of the bombing. Sometimes he thought his loneliness, his suffering was more than he could bear.

Outside a late autumn thunderstorm was sending the shutters crashing against the side of the house. As

Khalid had once told him, Cambria was a hovel of a castle. Gloomily Giles reflected that he would probably have been better off moving to the United States, as a nineteenth-century ancestor had—a black sheep, or so the story went.

The telephone rang, and, frustrated with the interruption, he rose to answer it. The crackle of static on the wires told him the call was long distance. It was his agent, with the news that *Out of the Darkness* had been sold, and for quite a bit of money.

Giles listened to the man explain the more tedious terms of the contract, then replaced the receiver, feeling slightly dazed. He wanted to share his astounding news with someone, but there was no one—not unless he counted Gwynfor, who continued to motor over for a visit every few days in hopes that he would change his mind about calling off their engagement.

She was as dauntless as Phillipa, but with none of Phillipa's quiet courage or complexity of mind and vast experience. An hour spent talking to Gwynfor and he was utterly bored.

He had spent thousands of dollars and weeks of time trying to track down the elusive Lady Phillipa Fleming. Invariably she seemed to stay just a step ahead of him. Once he found out that she had stayed a week in a leased *chaumière* near Biarritz. Sometimes she called Sigourney, or her brothers Guy and Robert, but none could pry her present location from her. At last, thoroughly discouraged, he had hired a detective to scour Europe for her, but with no results.

Well, if he couldn't share his excitement with Phillipa, he could at least tell Father Murphy, to whom he had sent a copy of the book.

Over the long distance line the irascible priest's voice was gruff, yet as warm as ever. "Giles, my son, glad you called. You were on my mind. How are you faring?"

"I suppose marvelously, Father. My agent just called and told me he had sold *Out of the Darkness* for enough money to keep Cambria in the black for a good while."

"Wonderful! I just finished that copy of the manuscript you sent me. It's going to be a bestseller, I assure you! We'll have Damon lionize you and make you the author laureate of Macedonia."

Giles chuckled. "I'm not Macedonian, Father, and I doubt there is such a thing as an author laureate."

"Well, don't refurbish Cambria yet. 'It takes the publishing industry so long to produce books that many are posthumous.' Don't ask me who said that. I can't remember."

Giles gathered his courage. "Then I'll ask you something else instead. Have you heard anything from Phillipa?"

"Strange you should ask. The Macedonian Religious Council had a meeting this last weekend, and you'd never believe who I ran into."

Giles's breath sucked in, but his hopes were quickly deflated as Father Murphy said, "No, not Phillipa— but listen, my son, why don't you catch the next flight out to Macedonia? With all the royalties you'll be getting on your book, you can easily afford it. When you get here, I'll fill you in.''

So this was what the Aegean looked like off the peninsula. Giles had envisioned it just so, with the white-foamed waves splashing against the glinting rocks at the base of the cliff. Phillipa had described it for him far better than any photo could have.

The wind was much cooler at this time of the year, but when he closed his eyes he could feel the sunlight warming his face. Strange, he thought, those months when he had been blind, he had learned how to really see.

There on the balcony of the little guesthouse the salt-tangy wind rushed in off the sea, swishing the cassock hems of the two men who flanked him.

''Beautiful!'' Father Stavroniketa marveled.

''Which?'' Father Murphy asked. ''The sea, or the woman sitting on the rocks?''

The monk's smile reflected the sunlight. ''Why, both.''

''Well, my son,'' Father Murphy said to Giles, ''don't you have better things to do than waste your time with two old celibates?''

In Giles's jaw a muscle flicked with trepidation. How could he ever convince Phillipa to see the same vision he did?

Father Murphy chuckled and said, '' 'He who hesitates is not only lost but miles from the next exit.' I don't know who said that, either. Now begone with you.''

Leaving the two on the balcony, Giles descended the stairs two at a time and hurried outside. The path leading to the cliffs was just as he had expected it, except that some of the trees were now bare.

At the brow of the cliff he paused. Far below, on a projecting ledge, sat Phillipa, her legs curled under her. She had always worn designer clothes, but this autumn afternoon she was wearing an olive-green ribbed cardigan and jeans—and she was reading a manuscript, the one Father Murphy had passed along to Father Stavroniketa.

The Lord *did* work in mysterious ways, Giles thought, as he began to wend his way down the narrow slope.

The noise of the wind and sea hid his approach, and he stood almost behind her before his shadow across the printed page betrayed his presence. Her head swerved upward, and he saw the tears glinting in her eyes. ''Giles!''

He hunkered beside her and lifted her chin. ''Why are you crying?''

''It's beautiful. Your story. It's about us, isn't it?''

''You read the dedication page, didn't you?''

She nodded. '' 'For the Wanted Woman.' ''

He brushed her lips with his, then said, ''That's not all of it. 'For the Wanted Woman—Phillipa, whom I love.' ''

Her lips quivered. ''Oh, Giles, are you certain?''

"I never was more certain of anything, my love."

"But when I'm sixty, you'll be just forty-six...in your prime."

"And when you're eighty-five, I'll be seventy-one. So what?"

"What about children? I can't give you—"

"Phillipa, love, there are too many Welsh children made orphans by mining accidents and disease. If we decide we want children, we can adopt some of them. They're the true bloodline of Cambria."

She shook her head. "I don't know. I just don't—"

"I do. I know that I won't ever let you leave me again."

"If you were willing to give up your possible sight—even your life—for me," she began hesitatingly, "...then perhaps there is a future for our love. Perhaps our age differences don't matter after—"

He didn't give her a chance to say another word. He convinced her in the only way he knew. In that one kiss he put all his soul and heart, all his past loneliness and emptiness, and all his need for her in his future.

On a balcony far above them Father Murphy said to the monk beside him, "'For the preservation of chastity, an empty and rumbling stomach and fevered lungs are indispensable.' St. Jerome said that. Fortunately, he didn't rule out consecrated wine. St. Nicolas wouldn't happen to have any on its premises, would it, Father Stavroniketa?"

The monk laid a companionable arm over the ugly old priest's shoulders. "No, but the monastery does have a precious cache of pungent herbal liqueur. You might find it a trifle potent.''

"I doubt it. Regardless, I suspect we shall soon need it to toast a long-overdue wedding.''

Silhouette Intimate Moments

COMING NEXT MONTH

#193 KISS OF THE DRAGON—Barbara Faith

Her dying father's request brought Bethany Adams to Hong Kong. There, Tiger Malone swept Bethany up in a hunt through China, where they risked their lives to find a golden dragon and discovered a greater treasure—love.

#194 LEGACY—Maura Seger

Gwen Llywelyn came to Wales to see her ancestral home, but she found much more: mysterious tremors and power failures—and Owen Garrett. Owen wasn't exactly who he said he was, but Gwen quickly decided he was all she'd ever wanted.

#195 THE GENUINE ARTICLE—
Katheryn Brett

A. J. McMichaels expected life in her small hometown to be uneventful, not sizzling with rumors of political corruption. She didn't expect to find herself feuding with the mayor, Rich Beckman, either—and she certainly didn't expect to fall in love with him.

#196 GYPSY DANCER—Kathleen Creighton

For Lily Fazekas, going to Hungary was a romantic quest for the family she had never known. Joseph Varga's assignment was to stay with her until the search was over, but long before that time arrived, he knew he wanted to stay with her—forever.

ATTRACTIVE, SPACE SAVING BOOK RACK

Display your most prized novels on this handsome and sturdy book rack. The hand-rubbed walnut finish will blend into your library decor with quiet elegance, providing a practical organizer for your favorite hard-or soft-covered books.

Only $9.95

Approximately 16" x 8" when assembled

Assembles in seconds!

To order, rush your name, address and zip code, along with a check or money order for $10.70* ($9.95 plus 75¢ postage and handling) payable to *Silhouette Books*.

Silhouette Books
Book Rack Offer
901 Fuhrmann Blvd.
P.O. Box 1325
Buffalo, NY 14269-1325

Offer not available in Canada.

*New York residents add appropriate sales tax.

BKR-2R

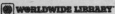